Kip Campbell's Gift

The Funeral Director's Son

Kip Campbell's Gift

Coleen Murtagh Paratore

SIMON & SCHUSTER BOOKS FOR YOUNG READERS
NEW YORK LONDON TORONTO SYDNEY

SIMON & SCHUSTER BOOKS FOR YOUNG READERS
An imprint of Simon & Schuster Children's Publishing Division
1230 Avenue of the Americas, New York, New York 10020

For information about special discounts for bulk purchases, please contact Simon & Schuster Special Sales at 1-866-506-1949 or business@simonandschuster.com.
The Simon & Schuster Speakers Bureau can bring authors to your live event. For more information or to book an event, contact the Simon & Schuster Speakers Bureau at 1-866-248-3049 or visit our website at www.simonspeakers.com.
Book design by Lucy Ruth Cummins
The text for this book is set in Berkeley.
Manufactured in the United States of America
10 9 8 7 6 5 4 3 2 1
Library of Congress Cataloging-in-Publication Data
Paratore, Coleen, 1958–
Kip Campbell's gift : the funeral director's son / Coleen Murtagh Paratore.—1st ed.
p. cm.
Sequel to: The funeral director's son.
Summary: Still able to hear the voices of dead people who want him to help them with unresolved problems, Kip Campbell struggles with conflicting feelings about his unique ability and the burdens it places on him in his daily life.
ISBN 978-1-4169-3596-4 (alk. paper)
ISBN 978-1-4169-9633-0 (eBook)
[1. Undertakers and undertaking—Fiction. 2. Funeral homes—Fiction.
3. Dead—Fiction. 4. Family life—Massachusetts—Fiction.
5. Massachusetts—Fiction.] I. Title.
PZ7.P2137Kj 2009
[Fic]—dc22
2008027073

To my wonderful son Connor,

who has so many gifts.

Love forever,

Mom

Contents

Kip Campbell's Gift

CHAPTER 1

King of the Sea

All this and heaven too.

—Matthew Henry, 1662–1714

I'm going to tell you straight out, I hear voices.

Not the regular kind everybody hears. These voices are in my head.

It's a talent, or a torture. I'm not sure which.

Some days I feel like a hero. Some days I feel like a freak. It all depends on the day.

Who do I hear talking?

Sometimes it's people who just died here in Clover.

Sometimes it's God, or at least I *think* it is.

Sometimes it's my own voice talking to me. Kip Campbell talking to Kip.

Right now, though, all I hear is the wind whistling loud in my ears. I'm sitting up here on my throne, way high up on Clover Cliff. It's not really a throne; I'm no king. It's more like a chair carved out naturally in the rocks. Up here it's just me and the sky and that big blue whippin' wild Atlantic Ocean. I come here to figure things out.

To get to this spot I crawl out over the sea wall mountain-climber style. It's easy until the last smooth boulder which doesn't have a crevice to get a toehold on; I've nearly slipped in the drink a dozen times, and then, one quick leap and I'm in.

It's like my own secret cave here, except, I told you, it's a throne. When I was a little kid and I first discovered this place, I'd wear my superhero cape and hold up a stick to rule the seagulls. Those birds flew when they saw me. I was Neptune, King of the Sea. Tell anybody that and you're dead. Just kidding.

I shouldn't joke about the dead. My father—he's a funeral director—would say that was disrespectful. Our family runs Campbell and Sons Funeral Home. We live upstairs from the business. Family on the second floor. Funerals on the first. Frankenstein stuff in the basement. Oooh, scary. No, not really. Somebody's got to do this line of work. Dad says it's more than a profession, it's a sacred calling. If that's true, don't call me. Being a funeral director is the last thing I want to be.

Everybody in my family has a job with the business. Me, I'm the Outdoor Guy. I mow, rake, shovel, and handle the parking lot. I also have another job my family and friends don't know about. I help the dead rest in peace.

I don't help all the dead in Clover, just the ones with anchors weighing them down. Something important they needed to do or say. They can't move on until that burden is gone. That's where I come in. The dead tell me what they need and I take care of it. I'm sort of like their fairy godbrother without the wings and glitter.

When I do my job well, the anchors are lifted and then the dead are free as birds, light as kites, ready to sail to Good. That's what I call heaven. Good.

Now, I know you know what life is because you're reading this and so, guess what, you're alive. Congratulations. As to what Good is . . . well, that's a slipperier fish.

I'm not sure about angels and saints and pearly gates, but I'm pretty certain that if you live your life right, you get to go to Good.

*

There's a green shamrock on the sign when you enter our town, Clover, Massachusetts. My grandmother, Nanbull, says the three petals on the clover remind us why we're here:

To live.

To love.

To leave something better behind.

Simple, huh? But simple can be hard. When dead people from Clover can't move on, it's usually because something's troubling them in one of those three simple areas. It's my job to help them wrap things up so they can go in peace.

That's what everybody says at a funeral: "May the dearly departed rest in peace."

Personally, I don't think the dead rest at all. I think once the funeral's over and the family's headed off to the potluck buffet lunch, the dead person sets sail to something better. When they open their eyes, they're right smack in the center of their best birthday ever, with everything they've ever wanted and all the people they love and meatball subs and chocolate shakes never running out and they're so whippin' happy and the feeling never ends. I think that's what heaven is. Your personal idea of good.

Just a few weeks ago I was all set to give up this job

with the dead. I didn't ask for it and I don't know why I got picked. I'm just an average kid. Good-looking, but average. At first it was fun and I felt pretty decent about myself helping dead dudes move on. But then this work started mucking up my life. I'd never know when a dead one would start yakking in my head. Like, I'd be in center field with the bases loaded and the ball soaring sweet for my mitt and it's all mine, all mine, when some dead lady starts telling me her problem and my brain freezes and I lose my focus and my buddies are screaming, "The ball, Kip, the ball!!" Or, in history class when my teacher called on me for an answer and some dead guy started talking and I shouted, "Not now!" and my teacher thought I was dissing her.

And not to mention I was doing all this dead-work for free. I kept saying I needed to get a real job, one that paid money so I could save for the Nauset Whaler down at Maloney's Marina I've been eyeing since I could see.

Finally, I gave notice. I was done. Finished, kaput. *Hasta la vista*, baby.

Then Billy Blye died.

I'd been afraid of that mean old fisherman my whole life. I refused to help. No way. He could be anchored here forever for all I cared.

Then I heard the most incredible words:

Do this work for one more year and it will be worth your weight in gold.

At first I thought, *no way, what a scam. Do you think I'm a fishbrain or what?*

Then, believe it or not, I found gold nuggets on the beach and took them to this pawn shop, Clover Stamp and Coin, and guess what? They were worth $1,180! Enough for me and Tuck to go to Camp Russell this summer like we've always wanted.

I figured maybe those nuggets were appetizers. Little franks in blankets with mustard dipping sauce before the gigundo roast beef dinner.

I calculated it all out and if I gain just twenty more pounds between now and next October, when I get my weight in gold, I'll be almost a millionaire. Pretty sweet, huh?

My heart's pounding just thinking about it. With that kind of dough, Tuck, Stew, Jupe, and I would never have to work a day in our lives. We could sail our mega–souped-up Nauset Whaler around the globe like those millionaire dudes on TV, living the good life forever.

You're thinking what the heck's my problem,

right? Gold sounds good to you. The thing is . . . I want to know where the gold came from. I can't stop wondering. This lady in Clover, Birdie O'Shaughnessy, held out something sparkly to show me one day on the beach. Was that gold? Did she put it there? Or maybe God did? Or was it from that old sunken pirate ship they're excavating off the coast of Cape Cod? Where did the gold come from? I need to know.

All will be revealed in time.

I jump at the voice inside me, nearly fall off my throne.

A deal's a deal, Kip. You agreed. Help the dead for one more year and it will be worth your weight in gold.

CHAPTER 2

The Christophers

. . . Heaven has no favorites.

—Lao-tzu, c. 604–c. 531 B.C.

Biking home from the beach for dinner, I spot a hawk perched high in a tree, gray-hooded and creepy like a medieval monk. That old gawker will wait, still as a statue, until the perfect moment, when it will *pounce,* sinking its talons deep into squirming fresh rodent flesh. That poor mouse won't even see it coming.

It's the end of October, getting colder; the first frost was last night. Fat brown oak and orange maple leaves are falling in front of my face, crackling under my tires, swirling up around me as I ride. I'll be raking the yard all weekend at this rate. We don't have one of those monster machines that sucks up leaves like a vacuum. I do it the old–fashioned way, with a rake.

Everybody in our family has a job with Campbell and Sons. My dad handles all the funeral arrangements. Mom manages the office. Uncle Marty is our embalmer. He prepares the body of the deceased for viewing. His wife, my Aunt Sally, does hair and makeup. My grandmother, Nanbull, writes the obituaries and funeral programs. Great Aunt Aggie's our musician. My annoying big sister, Lizbreath, does flowers. She breathes on them and they die. Just kidding. My little sister, Chick, is cool; she basically just giggles. Me, well, I already told you. I've got two jobs.

That's my house there on the corner of Piper and Glenn, the tall red-brick one with the green-canvas awnings and the black iron fence and the sign CAMPBELL AND SONS FUNERAL HOME SINCE 1875. Dad says it's one of the oldest houses in Clover, "grand in its day." *Honk, honk,* a vee of geese sails over me, off to a sunnier place. I look at our crumbling chimney, the roof shingles in need of repair. It doesn't look grand anymore.

When I unlock the front door, the scent of flowers and furniture polish washes over me like fog on the beach. The first floor, the funeral floor, is eerily quiet; the viewing room is empty, lights off in the office and parlor. No viewing tonight.

The long line of gold-framed Christophers stare solemnly out at me as I pass by. Six generations of funeral directors. There's the portrait of my father, Christopher Francis Campbell. My grandfather, Christopher Edmund Campbell. My great-grandfather, Christopher Desmond Campbell. All the way back to the original, Christopher Addison Campbell, one grim-looking dude if you ask me. Six proud Christophers in a row, with an empty space on the wall for the face of number seven. Everyone assumes that will be me.

Seven is supposed to be a lucky number. It doesn't feel lucky to me. I know it's my father's dream to pass on the funeral home to me. That's what the Christophers do. They pass along the business in a never-ending chain like royalty, father to son, father to son. That chain would anchor me here for good.

It's not that I don't love my family or my town. No, I've got the best family in the world and Clover's a good enough place to live. It's just that I don't want to be a funeral director and if I stay I'll have to. It would break my father's heart if I didn't.

I want to have a normal life, come and go as I please, without worrying about somebody dying and their loved one calling, waking you up in the middle of the night. I want to be free of all that. Too heavy an anchor, if you ask me.

The problem is that it will hurt my dad so bad if I don't follow in his footsteps. He's so proud of this business. It's his family's legacy. Everything he's worked for, every day of his life. Campbell and Sons Funeral Home. Seven generations proud.

You don't break a link in a chain that strong.

Not without consequences.

CHAPTER 3

The Cowboys

There's a tree that grows in Brooklyn.
Some people call it the Tree of Heaven.
No matter where its seed falls, it makes a tree
which struggles to reach the sky.

—Betty Wehner Smith, 1904–1972

Upstairs, Mom and Dad are in the kitchen, bills spread out between them on the table, radio turned to the Red Sox game. We've got a real shot at the series this year. Mom's tapping keys on a calculator.

"We need another loan," she says.

Dad shakes his head. "No, Evelyn, we—" Dad sees me and stops talking. He starts stuffing the bills in a folder.

Mom smiles at me. She stands up and moves toward the stove. "How was school, Kip?" she says all cheery, like everything is fine. She puts a skillet on the stove and pours in some oil.

"Okay," I say. "Any funeral calls today, Dad?"

"No, son," he says sadly.

Dad isn't as smooth as Mom about covering his worries with a smiley face. The fat pockets under his big brown eyes are drooping low like a hound dog's. Golden's, the new deluxe funeral home that just opened in town, is stealing away our business, big-time. They've got four huge viewing rooms, two chapels, a theater for showing memorial video tributes, a gigantic parking lot with fountains out front, and a fleet of sleek black limousines. They've got money to burn on advertising. I'm sick of seeing that Golden guy on the television screen every night, looking like he's a saint, like he really cares about Clover families. He doesn't know us. He's not from here. My grandmother, Nanbull, says Golden's is part of a huge national chain. They're gobbling up little guys like Campbell's for breakfast. Nanbull calls them the cowboys.

Our business is down, way down. That's bad. Not that we want anybody to die. Of course not. But no funerals, no income, it's as simple as that. The fall is usually a busy season. Once you hit Thanksgiving and then Christmas, the death rate drops off. Somehow the dying manage to hang in there until January. It's like they try hard to give their families one last nice holiday gift. I don't know how they do it, but they do. It's really pretty thoughtful of them, actually.

"You need a haircut, Kip," Dad says, tapping above his ear, to show the appropriate length.

"I'm all right, Dad." I flick my hair off my forehead. I like my hair. It's dark brown and shiny and it flips off all shaggy on the ends. The best thing is that it's finally long enough to cover my big ears, and the bangs are good camouflage from teacher eyes—like in math today. We're doing a section on Algebra. I usually ace math, but Algebra's a different animal, mixing up numbers with letters; that doesn't seem right.

"No, it's not all right, Christopher," Dad says, still talking about my hair. "It doesn't look professional."

"Come on, Dad. I'm not a professional. I'm a kid. Everybody's hair is long."

"I'm not everybody's father," Dad says in a tired but calm voice.

My dad's not a shouter. He's built like a linebacker, the biggest guy in Clover, but I've never seen him throw his weight around or even lose his cool. I don't think he has one mean bone in his big old body. He's like an oversized teddy bear with a giant heart to match. Everybody loves my dad.

Mom tosses garlic into the pan and it sizzles, smelling good. "We're having spaghetti and meatballs," she says, trying to change the subject away from hair. My Mom is so nice too. Everybody loves my mom. I lucked out in the parents department.

"Mom, make some extra meatballs for subs, okay?"

One excellent thing about our lack of funeral business is that Mom can make real dinners involving pots and pans and ovens and recipes. On nights when there is a viewing downstairs, we have cold sandwiches and salad. You can't have food aromas wafting down like a restaurant during somebody's calling hours. Although with all those stinking carnations and lilies people send from the florist, I don't know how you could smell anything else anyway.

Those flowers give me a headache. They make me want to puke. The smell sinks into my hair and clothes like some old dude's cologne. I can't get away from those flowers. They haunt me. When Dad needs my help with a morning funeral and I don't have time to change my suit before school, I reek like flippin' funeral flowers all day long.

"Hey, Flower Boy," that fish-gut Bub Jeffers or his lamebrain friend Dirk Hogan will shout, like they're being original although they've been calling me "Flower Boy" and "Deadbo" for years, and then their friends on the Clover Clarions will crack up laughing. I hate Bub Jeffers. Someday I'm going to get even with him.

"Don't listen to Bub," Tia Benson said to me in science a few weeks ago. "I like how you smell, Kip, and you look *good* in that suit."

My best friend Tucker says Tia's got a crush on me. That might be so, and Tia is cute, but I've got my eyes on—

"I mean it, son," Dad says again. "Please get a haircut before church Sunday."

"Kip," Mom says, always the peacekeeper, "would you please get Chick? She's been upstairs all afternoon. I bet Nanbull and Aunt Aggie could use a break."

"Sure, Mom," I say, glad to get away.

CHAPTER 4

Druelove 13

No act of kindness,
no matter how small,
is ever wasted.

from *The Lion and the Mouse*, Aesop, 550 B.C.

My grandmother and Aunt Aggie live in the attic.
Nanbull calls it the Senior Suite. When I knock on
the door, I hear giggling. That would be my little
sister, Chick. She's three.

Nanbull answers the door. "There's my favorite
grandson," she says, all happy to see me. She gives
me a hug.

Just for the record, I'm her only grandson, but
even if Nanbull had ten, I bet I'd still be her favorite
one. We're pretty tight like that.

"I'm glad you came, Kip," Nanbull says, winking.
"Aunt Aggie and I have a *big problem*. We lost Chick!

We've looked high and low, but she's disappeared. We're so worried we were about to call the police. Can you please help us find her?"

I hear a giggle from behind Nanbull's blue chair.

Aunt Aggie is sitting in the other blue chair, feet up on the ottoman, bundled up in a blanket, knitting. She's been sick for a while now and doesn't seem to be getting better.

"How you doing, Aunt Ag?" I say.

She adjusts her hearing aid. "Good, Kip. What's the score?"

She means the Red Sox game. "Bottom of the fifth; Sox up two."

"That's right," Aunt Ag says, pumping her knitting needle in the air, "we're going all the way, baby, all the way!" She goes back to knitting her mouse lady with new enthusiasm.

Aunt Aggie is famous in Clover for her mouse ladies. People use them to cover spare rolls of toilet paper in the bathroom. The ladies wear long ruffly dresses, floppy hats, and hand-warmers. Aunt Ag sells them at church bazaars and craft fairs.

Personally, I don't see a problem with naked toilet paper, but I'm not saying anything. If it makes Aunt Aggie happy, that's cool.

The mouse ladies carry little signs:

IF YOU SPRINKLE WHEN YOU TINKLE,

PLEASE BE NEAT AND WIPE THE SEAT.

I hear Chick laughing again. "Sure, Nanbull," I say, "I'll help you find Chick, but I've got to sit down a minute. I'm tired."

I plop down hard on Nanbull's chair and push the arm forward to make the back recline all the way.

"Hey! Watch out," Chick shrieks, then giggles hysterically.

I reach my hand around to grab Chick and pull her up on my lap. "Come here, you." She's lighter than a bag of leaves.

"Don't tickle me, Kip, don't tickle me," Chick says. Which of course means *tickle me, tickle me more*.

Chick has a job with the family business too. She's our official giggler. She sticks little red, yellow, blue, or green smiley face stickers on people during calling hours and that generally makes them laugh, which is a pretty good thing in a funeral home.

When Chick's had her fill of tickles, she scoots off my lap and makes a mean eye-squinting face. She reaches her hand in the pocket of her deerskin cowgirl vest, then points her little pink water pistol at me.

"Hands up, pardner. I'm taking you in."

Chick watches way too many old movies in the Senior Suite. Somebody ought to take this kid to the mall.

"Yes, ma'am," I say, putting my hands way up in the air, shaking like I'm scared.

"Sheriff Campbell to you," Chick says, pointing to her silver badge. She smoothes the fringes of her skirt and cocks down the corner of her hat. She makes like she's tying my hands up with a rope. "Now let's git a move on, before the sun goes down and the vultures'll pluck your eyeballs out."

I try to look petrified as I walk to the door. "Can I get one more meal before you lock me up, Sheriff? I smell meatballs cooking."

Chick giggles and pokes me in the butt with her pistol. "Maybe," she says. "Move."

Nanbull winks at me as I pass by. "You're such a good brother," she whispers.

I walk down the stairs to our floor, hands high under arrest, smelling the plaster where the old green and yellow flowered wallpaper is peeling. I think about Dad telling me to get a haircut. It's my hair. I'm almost thirteen. Dad can't treat me like a baby anymore. I push open our door. *Hmm.* Meatballs. Life is good.

And it gets even better. When I go online after dinner to check my messages, there's one from Druelove 13. That's Drew Callahan, the new harbormaster's daughter. She's beautiful. I think I'm in love with Druelove. I feel bad, though, because I told her a big lie when she moved into Clover. She acted spooked when she found out I lived in a funeral home, so I said we were selling the business and that my father was opening up a sports complex and we were moving to a new house soon. I need to set her straight.

Drew wants to know what I'm going to be for Halloween. She wants me to go trick-or-treating with her. *Sweet.*

My computer beeps. It's Drew again. She asks why I'm not answering her.

What can I be for Halloween? No clue.

I type: **What R u gonna be?**

A soccer player, she says.

Okay, so she's playing it safe. I type: **Me 2. U stole my idea.**

She says, **Ha. Ha. Let's go as a team. What position do you play?**

Striker, I say.

Me 2, she says.

Sounds good, I say.

Gotta go, Dad's home, she says, and signs off.

Wait until I tell Tuck. He'll be mad that I'm blowing him off. We always do Halloween together. But he'll understand for sure.

Drew signs back on again: **PS I love your hair.**

Thanx, I type, and sign off.

I check out my face in the mirror. No way am I cutting my hair.

I read for a while and then shut my light off. I close my eyes picturing Drew Callahan's beautiful smile and how her whole face lights up when she's laughing.

No *way* am I cutting my hair.

CHAPTER 5

Heaven is under our feet as well as over our heads.

—Henry David Thoreau, 1817–1862

TGIF. Thank God it's Friday.

Friday morning, like every school day, I go to meet my friends at the corner. Tucker, my best friend, is there first, like always. When he sees me, he shuts off his gamebox and tucks it in his backpack, embarrassed.

Jupe and Stew and I have graduated to cellphones, but Tuck's still playing kid games. His parents won't buy him a phone. They can't afford it. Mine wouldn't have either, except for the business. You never know when a call is going to come in and we all have to do our jobs. The funeral business isn't like running a grocery store or a bakery, with regular hours and closing times.

If a family needs Campbell and Sons, they can call us anytime and count on us to be open. Every day that ends in y, morning, noon, or night.

Ever since kindergarten, people used to say Tuck and I looked like brothers. We're both tall and skinny with blue eyes and dark brown hair, but now Tuck's got bad acne and glasses and his mom cuts his hair weird, and his pants are always two inches too short, trying to make them last another year.

"Hey, Kip," Tuck says. "Guess what! Tia Benson wants to go out with you on Halloween. She called me last night saying how good-looking you are and how smart and funny you are and how you've got hair like a rock star. Why do girls tell me all this stuff, anyway?"

"Cause you're so lovable," I say.

"Shut up," Tuck says. "I am lovable, though. I'd take some love, anytime. Anyway, Tia likes you, dude. She *like* likes you. She said to tell you she wants to go out with you and if you want to, give her a call. Tia's hot, man. You're lucky."

"Yeah, but I like somebody else."

"Who?"

"Drew."

"*Drew Callahan*." Tuck shakes his head in awe.

"You're talking top shelf at the arcade now. She's fine. But does she like *you*?"

"Yeah, I guess so. We were online last night and she asked me to go trick-or-treating on Halloween."

"*Luck-ee*," Tuck says, sliding his broken glasses with the Band-Aid holding the frame together back up on his nose. "You've got the two cutest girls in the class fighting over you. Come on, Kip. Share the wealth. Split that candy bar with me."

Our friends Stew and Jupey bike around the corner and we all head off to school.

"You got enough lunch there?" I say to Stew. He's hauling a pack big enough to feed our whole class. Stew's mother, Mrs. Brumbaugh, runs the Bumblebee Diner, home of the best cheeseburgers, chili-cheese fries, clam chowda', and chocolate layer cake this side of the Bourne Bridge. Cape Cod's got nothing on Clover's Bumblebee.

"Shut up, Kip," Stew says. "We need stuff for Guts and Mom sent in brownies for Mrs. Clark's birthday."

"Ooooh," Jupe teases. "Stewie's got some brown-nosing brownies for the science teacher. Mrs. Clark will be saying, 'Stewart. You did earn a disappointing

D on your last quiz, but with these brownies . . . *mmm, mmm,* they're good. Let's see what I can do. I know! I'll just add a little line in the middle of that letter, and *look*, now that D's a B!"

"No fair, Stew," Tuck says. "Give me the brownies. I flunked that test. I need them more than you do."

Tuck has got to be really careful that he doesn't fail any of his main courses or they'll hold him back a grade. They almost did last year, but he squeezed through at the end. We did some all-nighters together to get him ready for exams. Then Nanbull proofed his final essay for English and helped Tuck "pull some more good ideas" out of his head.

Tuck's got a lot of good ideas, he just has a few "learning challenges," too. He's as smart as the next guy, but sometimes he forgets to read directions or doesn't realize there are questions on the other side of the test page too, and some teachers don't cut him any slack. Mrs. Clark, she's cool, but back in third grade we had this teacher who kept asking "Are you stuck again, Tucker?" and then some kid called Tucker "Stucker," and, well, kids have been calling him that ever since.

Names have a way of sticking like that. My dad has

a friend named "Tuna." The guy's real name is Michael Murray. He's a big-shot businessman in Boston, but all his Clover buddies at the Lodge still call him "Tuna" when he comes home to visit. Where'd he get the name Tuna? I asked my dad. Dad said he had no idea, couldn't remember. "He's just Tuna, that's all."

We get to school and park our bikes. Bub Jeffers and Dirk Hogan, the biggest guys in our class, Loser Number 1 and Loser Number 2, are tossing a football with some tall blond kid I've never seen before.

"That's Campbell right there," Bub says to the blond kid, pointing over at me. "The one with the long hair."

I walk toward them. I have no choice. There's only one entrance door.

"Hey, Flower Boy," Bub shouts to me. "Come meet your competition."

Stew, Jupe, Tuck, and I advance like a defensive lineup.

"Oh yeah," I say, smoothly, "who's that?" I'm thinking this new kid likes Drew or Tia or maybe both of them.

The new kid steps forward and sticks out his chin. He's tall and chunky, with dyed yellow hair, black around the roots.

"I'm Zack Golden," he says, accentuating the last name. "My uncle owns Golden's Funeral Home. You know, Campbell, the place that's going to squash your mom-and-pop shop like a can of chicken soup."

Bub and Dirk crack up laughing

"Good one, Zack," Bub says. "Campbell's soup. I didn't think about that."

"Stick with me," Zack says. "I'll teach you kids a few things, shake this place up." Zack looks back at me. "So how's business, Campbell? Heard you're having some hard times."

"Who you talking to, loser?" my best friend Tuck says, coming up next to me.

Zack looks at Tuck and laughs. "Where'd you get those glasses?" he says.

Jupe moves forward and sticks his chest out, strong from pumping iron. Jupe stares down Zack Golden like Zack's a bug that just needs a good stomping. Jupe doesn't say a word. Jupe doesn't have to.

"Yeah, who are you talking to?" Stew pipes up, standing safely behind Jupe.

The bell rings and Mrs. O'Brien, our principal, opens the door all cheerfully and kicks down the doorstop. "Good morning, everyone."

We file in.

Drew Callahan smiles at me in Math, which sort of takes the edge off Algebra. Tia Benson drops a pack of Skittles on my desk and giggles as she passes by me in English. Everybody knows that's my favorite candy. "Thanks," I say.

Tia smiles, all happy. "I'll bring you some Monday, too."

The final bell rings. TGIF. Tuck, Stew, and I bike to Guts, our private clubhouse, up in Willow Grove Cemetery. It used to be the groundskeeper's cottage, but now it's abandoned, hidden behind a huge granddaddy of a willow tree. Jupe's getting a haircut. He's coming later.

I bike past the rows of headstones, mostly gray square blocks of marble with a family name engraved in the center. *Conroy. Gallagher. Buckley. Goodale.* Some are fancier than others, with crosses or angels on top. Some rich families even have their own mausoleums with benches outside like a park.

There's a freshly turned plot of black dirt with a mass of funeral flowers on top and then another farther down and a third one a few rows over. Brand new burials. They weren't ours. Golden's must have handled those calls. I think about Zack Golden.

A breeze blows and I hear a jangling sound coming from one of the headstones. It's a homemade wind chime. Forks and spoons, a soup ladle, and an old tin campfire mug dangling on strings, orange and yellow jingle shells and oyster shells glued on like decorations, a bright red bow on top. The wind blows again, harder this time, and the objects dance about in the air, crashing into each other gently, making a strange, sweet-sounding music. I stop to read the name on the marker. *Beatrice Jackson, 1928–1993.*

Nice spot you got here, Beatrice.

When we get to Guts, we push away the willow fronds and unlock the padlock.

Tuck turns on the old battery-operated lanterns his dad gave us from his fishing boat, and I grab three cans of soda from the icebox, our antique refrigerator. Nanbull gave it to us. People used to keep their food cold in these with blocks of ice before electricity was invented. The soda's warm, but we don't care.

Tuck deals a round of poker and Stew tears open a fresh bag of Oreos. I start packing them in, hoping to gain more weight.

"Hey, Campbell." We hear a shout from outside the door. "How many dead bodies ya got in there today?"

Tuck and Stew laugh.

It's Jupe pretending to be Bub Jeffers. Jeffers is always asking how many dead bodies I've got at my house.

"Yeah, I'm in here, Jeffers," I shout. "Come on in and I'll embalm ya."

Jupe pushes open the door with a big smile on his face.

"Where'd your hair go?" I say.

Jupe got another buzz cut, just like his dad. Jupe's father's a cop, the first black sergeant in Clover. My dad says that promotion was long overdue. Jupe and his dad are wicked close. Jupe's mom lives in California. He keeps hoping she'll come back, but I think that's a real long shot. Jupe and his dad spend lots of time together though, lifting weights, watching games, cruising around in the patrol car.

"I donated it to Locks of Love," Jupe says with a smirk, sliding his hand over his scalp. "Figured if my head got cold this winter, I'd just borrow some hair off you, Campbell. When you gonna get that cut, anyway? You look like a mop."

"But the *ladies* love it," Tuck says. "Tell them, Kip. He's got two girls fighting over him like cats."

"My mother says that's sexist," Stew says, his

cheeks bulging with cookies, "saying girls fight like cats."

"Get a life, Stewball," Jupe jokes, pulling the bag of Oreos out of Stew's hands. Jupe unscrews a cookie and scrapes the frosting off with his teeth. We always have Oreos and soda at Guts, plus whatever Stewie's mother sends from the Bumblebee.

"Oh, wait, I forgot," Stew says, reaching into his pack. "We've got brownies left too." He puts the plastic container on the table and I grab one. *Hmm.* I'm doing great on calories today. Every ounce is golden.

Tuck shuffles and deals another hand of poker.

"Hey, Kip," Stew says, "got any new ways to make money?"

The four of us are always trying to think of ways to make cash. Last summer we started this fast-food delivery service, Sun Runners, on Carey's beach, thinking people would pay us big tips to run up to the snack bar for them. We thought wrong. "Nah," I say. I think about the gold, but I'm not ready to tell my friends. It might get too complicated. And besides, I don't even know if I can tell anybody else.

"What about you, Jupe?" Stew says. "Any ideas?"

"My dad says Clover needs to figure out how

to get back all the tourist business we lost to Cape Cod. We need to reel in those sexy seniors with big pocketbooks out cruisin' on buses for adventure. We need a draw. You know, like that hot-dog eating contest they've got down in New York City or the chowder festival out on the Cape. I've been investigating online and wait till you hear this: The state of Washington's got a Cow Plop Raffle that draws in crowds like gold."

I perk up at the word "gold."

"What the heck's a cow plop?" Tuck says.

"Poop," Jupe says. "Cow poop, you know, like that big squishy brownie Stew's shoving in his mouth right now."

"How's the raffle work?" I ask.

"Easy," Jupe says. "The guys who run it make this huge bingo board, marking off hundreds of little white square boxes, in the biggest Wal-Mart parking lot they've got out there. Then they bring in this lucky cow named Miss Lilly and they plunk her down in the middle of the lot. You pay twenty bucks to buy a square. And then you wait and see."

"Wait and see what?" Stew says.

"Where Lilly plops," Jupe says. "If she craps on your square, you're the winner."

"Cool," Tuck says.

"Yeah, I told you it was good," Jupe says. "The winner gets a cut, and the organizers—that would be us—pocket the rest. Piece of cake."

"But we don't have a cow," Tuck says.

"Kip's got a cat," Stew says.

"Yeah," Jupe says. "That's good. We'll call it Clover's Cat Crap Contest."

"Something to think about," I say, imagining what my father would say about that.

We play three more rounds and then do rock-paper-scissors for the last brownie. Jupe wins, like always. Jupe's the RPS champ. He shoves it in his mouth and chews.

"That's cow plop, you know," Stew says.

"That's right," Jupe smiles, chewing. "Best cow plop this side of the Bourne Bridge."

We close up the icebox, turn off the lanterns, and head outside. It's cold and dark.

"Hey, Kip," Jupe says. "That Zack Golden dude was down at the barbershop getting his fake blond hair trimmed. When he left, I heard somebody say his parents are dead, got killed in a plane crash. Zack's been in foster homes his whole life because none of his relatives would adopt him. Finally his two uncles flipped a coin. The uncle who owns Golden's Funeral Home lost. That sucks, man, don't you think? Both your parents dead and nobody wants you and a flippin' quarter decides the whole rest of your life."

CHAPTER 6

"Freak"

A robin redbreast in a cage
Puts all Heaven in a rage.

—William Blake, 1757–1827

Dad is showered and dressed in one of his funeral director's suits next morning at breakfast. We must have gotten a call overnight. I'm sorry for whoever died, but I'm glad the family called us instead of Golden's.

Mom is making her famous chocolate chip pancakes. It's Saturday and I was going to sleep in before raking, but the smell of chocolate snuck under my door, hooked my nose, and yanked me right out here to the kitchen.

"She's finally out of her misery," Dad says to Mom. "It was a long time coming."

"They're loaded," Lizbreath says. "The daughter,

Majestic, she's a senior at my school. . . ."

Wait. I know that name, Majestic. . . .

"She's got her own car," Lizbreath is rambling on, "a Rolex, designer everything. They'll want top of the line, Dad. We're talking cash cow here. Let's milk it."

"Elizabeth!" Dad says, shocked. "Please don't speak so crassly about a family we may be serving."

"*May* be?" my mother says, pouring more batter on the griddle.

Dad sips his coffee, then sets down his favorite mug with the Massachusetts State Funeral Directors' Association logo on it. Dad was elected president of that group this year. It's a big deal. He's quite proud of that.

"Barry Jeffers was honest with me on the phone last night," Dad says. "He is interviewing Golden's at nine thirty and us at eleven o'clock. Nothing personal, he said. Just wants to know his options is how he explained it."

Jeffers? I put down my fork. "Is that Bub Jeffers's mother?"

Dad nods. "Yes, poor woman. She was in a nursing home—"

"That's cold," Lizbreath interrupts. "Why didn't

the family have her at home? They could have afforded a live-in nurse."

"That's enough, Liz," Mom says. "Who are we to judge?"

"It's *Lizbeth*," my sister says. She changed her name from Elizabeth to LIZ-beth, "accent on the first syllable," when she hit high school. I think she thinks Lizbeth sounds more sophisticated or something. Good luck.

"Listen to me, Elizabeth Campbell," Dad says, reaching out his arm to place his catcher's mitt-size palm on my sister's shoulder. "Not one word of this conversation is to leave this kitchen. Do you understand me? We have privacy agreements, a bond of trust with the families we serve."

"Yeah, yeah, I know, I know," Lizbreath says. "But this could be a really big call for us, Dad. We've got to put our best face forward."

"Well, you'll get your chance," Dad says. "Mr. Jeffers wants to meet the entire staff. I expect everyone dressed and downstairs in the front parlor at ten forty-five sharp. Kip, you don't have time to rake the whole yard, but at least do the walkway and sweep the porch."

"Sure, Dad, no problem." I finish chewing a

mouthful of pancakes which taste like Play-Doh now. I can't believe Bub Jeffers is coming here. I'm sorry he lost his mother, but . . .

I sweep the front walkway and steps, and then shower. I put on my white shirt, black suit, and tie. I dry my hair. It looks good. Now if I can just get Dad to forget about my cutting it, at least until my date—not a real date, just trick-or-treating with Drew.

We're sitting in the downstairs parlor, picture-perfect like one of those Norman Rockwell paintings in that museum in Stockbridge, listening to the *tick, tock, tick, tock* of the grandfather clock, when the doorbell rings just after eleven o'clock. Dad adjusts his tie and goes to answer it. I take a peppermint candy from the bowl, unwrap it quietly, and stuff the plastic in my pocket.

I hear my dad say, "Barry," to Mr. Jeffers. "Bud . . . Majestic, we are so sorry for your loss." And then there are some lines I can't hear. Dad says, "Please come this way. We're all waiting for you in the parlor."

When Bub sees me he sneers and turns away. Lizbreath, who actually looks fairly human when she dresses up nice, stands up like she runs the place. She walks over and shakes Bub's hand and then says something to Majestic.

Majestic starts crying and Lizbreath hugs her. Mom passes the tissue box.

We all sit down. Dad does the talking. Well, first, he listens. That's my dad's greatest strength. He listens with his big Boss Campbell ears and looks with his big Boss Campbell eyes, nodding and listening intently like he's got all day. And if it takes that long, so be it. "Never rush grief," Dad says.

He asks Mr. Jeffers how the family is doing and lets Mr. Jeffers tell the whole story about how awful this last year was and the toll it's taken on everyone, and when Mr. Jeffers is finally finished, Dad gently asks him if he has thought about what type of funeral arrangements he'd like.

Mr. Jeffers is prepared. He opens a black notebook. A fancy brochure slips out. He sticks it back in. Must be from Golden's. Mr. Jeffers wants two viewings, one in the afternoon, then a break, then another in the evening. A funeral Mass at St. Mary's the next morning. Interment at Willow Grove Cemetery. And do we do memorial movie tributes? And as for music . . .

"My mother loved pink," Majestic blurts out. "Her casket has to be pink."

Mr. Jeffers nods at his daughter. "Absolutely, sweetheart, anything you say."

"Yes, of course," Lizbreath says kindly. She stands up and goes to the shelf, lifts down the heavy leatherbound coffin catalog, and sits on the couch next to Majestic. I hear Dad clear his throat, loudly, but Lizbreath doesn't flinch. She opens the catalog to the section with the most expensive line of caskets, avoiding eye-contact with my dad. I know he would love to muzzle her right now.

Dad never tries to sell people overpriced caskets just to make more money. "The dead don't care what sort of coffin they're in," Dad says. "I'd rather see a family spend that money on the living, putting those dollars toward a kid's college fund or something."

"The mother-of-pearl is just the most elegant, I would venture to say, *royal*, shade of pink," Lizbreath gushes as if she's on that television shopping channel. "Truly worthy of a lady of distinction. Fit for a queen."

Dad clears his throat loudly again, trying to get Lizbreath to shut her trap, but my sister's just getting warmed up.

"And as for wardrobe considerations," Lizbreath

says, all poised and confident like she does this every day, when this is actually her funeral director debut—maybe *she* should take over the business—"knowing your impeccable taste in fashion, Majestic, let me show you this satin, mink-trimmed gown, perfect for these cool autumn evenings in Clover."

Majestic smiles and nods her head, her lips quivering like she's going to cry again. "Mother would have loved this," she says, reaching out to touch the sample fabric.

"Yes," Lizbreath nods her head in agreement. "And with your permission, Mr. Jeffers, I could special order it in from our designer in Paris and have it flown in tonight."

"Elizabeth!" Dad says. He smiles reassuringly at Majestic. "Liz," he says, lowering his voice, "would you kindly bring Mr. Jeffers some coffee?"

Lizbreath looks stunned, but recovers admirably. "Certainly, Father," she says. "How do you take your coffee, Mr. Jeffers?"

"Black, three sugars, thanks," Mr. Jeffers says.

Chick giggles. "*Three* sugars? That's bad. You're gonna get cavities."

Mother scoops Chick up in her arms. "Let's go help Liz with that coffee."

I can feel Bub's scornful eyes staring at me. Finally, I look at him. He sniffs the air like he's smelling farts. *Flowers.* I know he's dying to say "Flower Boy" but he can't very well say that here. He looks sneaky-quick to make sure no one sees him, then he waves his hands by his ears like Dumbo the flying elephant. He's aching to call me "Deadbo," too, but he can't do that sitting here. This is my house.

I hope Bub's hating me doesn't cost Dad this call. If the Jeffers family votes which funeral home to choose, us or Golden's, no question, Bub's picking the cowboys.

With a *meow*, my cat, Mosely, meanders in the room and heads straight for me. She must have snuck out when Lizbreath opened the door upstairs. Mosely is a black tuxedo cat, sleek black fur with white paws and chest, the smoothest, sliest cat you've ever seen.

"What's a friggin' cat doing here?" Bub says to his father.

Lizbreath comes in with the coffee tray and sets it on the table.

"Thank you, Liz," Dad says. "Now would you be so kind as to bring Mosely back upstairs?"

"But it's Kip's cat," she says politely to my father.

Liz hasn't even had a chance to talk about the new funeral jewelry line she suckered Dad into ordering from one of those funeral supply company salesmen she has a crush on.

"Thank you, Liz," Dad says. "But I would appreciate it if you would bring Mosely back upstairs."

I know Dad is mad and embarrassed that Liz keeps trying to sell things. Dad says people pay Campbell and Sons for the dignified, caring service we provide, not a bunch of products they don't need.

As she passes by me, Liz squints her eyes like *I'll get you for this.*

I unwrap another peppermint and pop it in my mouth. I listen as Dad and Mom and Uncle Marty and Nanbull talk with Mr. Jeffers about caskets and vaults and the service and music and the cemetery and the obituary and—

Tell Barry to marry Liza.

The lady's voice in my head startles me. The peppermint goes down the wrong way and I start to choke. I cough and cough. "Sorry," I say.

Barry. That's Mr. Jeffers name. This must be Mrs. Jeffers talking to me. Bub's mother is talking to me. I look around quickly. No one else hears her.

Tell Barry I was sick for so long and he took such good

care of me, but he needs to move on with his life now. Tell him I know how fond he is of Liza and I think he should marry her. . . .

No! I shout inside. I open another peppermint and chew, trying to block out her voice. Bub Jeffers's mother? No way.

Tell Barry I said Maj and Bub need a mother. Especially Bub.

I look at Mr. Jeffers. He's writing down notes. "Sounds good, Mr. Campbell," he says to Dad. "But I got to tell you, I'll need to think about this for a bit. Golden's has that big new theater. They'll do a whole movie about my wife and have it running during the viewings. They've got five stretch limos to transport all our relatives, and they showed us that same pink casket your daughter did, but it's ten percent cheaper, and they can . . ."

Tell him now, Kip. There may not be another chance. Tell Barry to marry Liza. She's a good woman. I worry about Bub, that boy's hurting inside. He's going to need a mother's love.

No! I shout back to her silently again. I don't want anything to do with Bub Jeffers. I hate that kid.

"Certainly," my father says to Mr. Jeffers. "Take all the time you need, Barry. I understand."

Why does my dad have to be so kind? Why isn't he trying to put a little pressure on Mr. Jeffers so that we get the call instead of Golden's? *Now, Kip, tell him. . . .*

Hey, wait a minute. What if telling Mr. Jeffers about his wife will win this call for my dad?

I stand up.

"Mr. Jeffers," I say, "could I speak with you out in the hallway for a minute? Privately."

Dad, Mom, Nanbull—their heads turn swiftly toward me in surprise.

I feel Bub's hateful eyes like two burning lasers on the side of my face, but I don't look his way. I might lose my nerve.

Mr. Jeffers shrugs his shoulders. "Sure," he says. "Why not."

Bub gets up to join us. "No," his father says. "Stay here with Maj."

I direct Mr. Jeffers into the viewing room and close the door so no one else can hear. I offer him a chair, but he refuses.

I take a deep breath. "I know this may be a shock to you," I say, "but your wife, Mrs. Jeffers, she asked me to tell you—"

"What?" Mr. Jeffers says, angrily. "When did you talk to my wife?"

"I know this may sound strange," I say. "But Mrs. Jeffers just spoke to me back there in the parlor."

Mr. Jeffers's face reddens. He stands and moves toward me, clenching his fist like he's going to punch me. "What kind of sick scam are you pulling here? Taking advantage of people when—"

"No, Mr. Jeffers." My heart is racing, sweat beading on my forehead. "Just hear me out, please. Your wife said to tell you that you did a great job taking care of her all those years that she was sick and now it's time for you to move on with your life. She says to marry Liza."

Mr. Jeffers's face freezes like he's in shock. He backs away from me.

"Mrs. Jeffers says that Liza is a good woman. She says to go ahead and marry Liza because Maj and Bub need a mother, especially Bub, because that boy's hurting inside and she's worried about him."

Mr. Jeffers makes a strangled sound, like a muffled scream, then collapses in a chair. He looks up at me like a little lost kid, then he puts his head in his hands and sobs.

My body is shaking. What do I do now? "I'm sorry," I say, touching his shoulder briefly then pulling my hand back. I stand there and let him bawl it all out.

Someone's knocking on the door.

Mr. Jeffers wipes his face and stands up. "I don't know how you know all this, kid, but thank you. You've just taken the weight of the world off my shoulders."

He cries again, but they seem like happy tears. "You probably want to know who Liza is," he says.

"No, sir, that's okay."

"You're entitled," Mr. Jeffers says. "Liza is my secretary. We never meant to fall in love, but Diane was so sick for so long and . . ." He shakes his head, clasps his hands together, and closes his eyes. "Thank you, Diane. I love you, honey."

When we join the others in the parlor, Bub goes immediately to stand next to his father. He starts to say something, but Mr. Jeffers cuts him off.

"I've made my decision," Mr. Jeffers says. "We're going with Campbell and Sons."

Dad moves toward him. They shake hands. Then Uncle Marty and Mom and Nanbull shake Mr. Jeffers's hand. Mom says something to Bub in a kind, quiet voice, and puts her hand on his arm. He pulls away like she's burned him.

At the door, Mr. Jeffers turns and says to my father, "That's quite a boy you've got there, Campbell." Mr.

Jeffers pats my shoulder. "That's a son you can be proud of."

Bub elbows me in the stomach as he passes by. "You're worse than a flower boy," he whispers. "You're a *freak*."

CHAPTER 7

The Blessing Bowl

*"There is a land of the living
and a land of the dead
and the bridge is love . . ."*

—Thornton Wilder, 1897–1975

As soon as the Jeffers family leaves, Dad and Mom ask me what I said to Mr. Jeffers. A part of me wants to tell them about the voices, but what if *they* think I'm a freak? Not to mention Lizbreath will be watching my every move even more.

"I reminded Mr. Jeffers that Golden's just opened last month, while the Campbells have been in Clover forever. People here are our neighbors, we know them. Most importantly, we knew Mrs. Jeffers, and we'd be honored to serve their family."

Dad gets misty-eyed. "Good, son," he says, patting his big bear mitt on my shoulder. "You get it,

Kip. This is what being a small-town funeral director is all about. Serving our neighbors with honor."

Mom looks at me with questioning eyes, but she doesn't spoil anything. "I'm proud of you, son," she says quietly. She looks at Dad and they smile.

"Good going, Kip," Nanbull says. "Tell Golden to put that in his pipe and smoke it."

Don't ask me. That's some old Irish thing Nanbull says. I'm not sure what it means, but it always makes me laugh. I think Nanbull knows a lot more about my hearing dead people then she's letting on.

When Mom and Dad leave the room Nanbull says, "Kip, wait. Is this like when you helped Billy Blye?"

"Yes."

"I knew it," she says, smiling. "You've got a gift, Kip."

The next day, Sunday, Dad is still so happy about getting the Jeffers call, that he completely forgets about my hair.

After we get home from Mass at St. Mary's, Dad and Mom sit at the kitchen table to work out the plans for Mrs. Jeffers's calling hours and funeral. Uncle Marty comes over for coffee, then says he's off to the hospital morgue to retrieve Mrs. Jeffers's body. Nanbull writes the obituary and sends it in to the *Clover Chronicle*. Lizbreath gets all upset when Dad tells her she may not, "under any circumstances," stop by the Jeffers to show them the new line of funeral jewelry.

"But Dad," she says.

"No."

"Please?"

"No."

Me, I spend the whole day raking leaves. I'm the Outdoor Guy.

Chick has a blast running and jumping into a leaf pile twice as tall as she is. Her fun makes more work for me, but that's okay. If a simple thing like a leaf pile can make Chick so happy, that's fine with me.

When Mom calls us in for dinner, my palms are red and my shoulders are aching. I bag the last pile and head in to take a shower, knowing full well more leaves will fall and blow over from Uncle Marty's property and I'll be back at it again next weekend.

Sunday dinner at the Campbells is like a holiday. Mom serves a nice meal at 2:00 p.m. and everyone has to dress nice. Since the Jeffers wake isn't until Tuesday because they're waiting on out-of-town relatives to fly in, Mom was able to use the stove. Good thing. Roast beef with gravy, mashed potatoes, brown-sugar–candied carrots, green beans, crescent rolls and two apple pies for dessert.

Nobody makes a better apple pie than my mom. I'd fight you on that. My nose is so happy it's dancing on my face and my mouth is watering like the ocean imagining how good this is all going to taste, but first we've got to do the stupid bowl.

Aunt Aggie gave the Blessing Bowl to Mom and Dad as a wedding gift. Mom keeps the silver bowl polished bright and takes it out of the china closet to use every Sunday. It's a Campbell family tradition.

Mom puts the Blessing Bowl on the table after church with a little stack of cards and some pens. Each person in the family is supposed to take a card and write one thing he or she is grateful for, one blessing, and then fold up the card and put it in the bowl before dinner. Now that Chick can count, she makes sure every person has a blessing in the bowl. Nanbull and Aunt Aggie are always included. I'm usually the last one in. It's not that I don't have things I'm grateful for, it's just I don't like writing about them.

We all take our favorite seats around the long oak

table, hand-carved by one of the first Christopher Campbells. The Campbells were originally carpenters by trade, making tables and chairs, cupboards and coffins, whatever their neighbors needed.

"Let's begin," Dad says.

We all hold hands—good thing Lizbreath always sits at the other end of the table, and we bow our heads. Today Aunt Aggie says grace. She has a thick, wooly sweater on over her dress, her silver hair in a donut-bun on her head. She starts to speak and then gets a fit of coughing. She nods at Nanbull and my grandmother takes over. I sneak a peak at Chick. She's looking at Aunt Aggie, worried. I squeeze Chick's hand. Chick looks at me. I wink at her and smile. She smiles back and closes her eyes.

Then, while the aroma of that succulent roast beef is tempting me to attack it with a fork right now, we have to go around the table and if anyone wants to share his or her blessing out loud, they can. If not, that's okay too. It's all in the bowl. The silver bowl sitting between the fluffy mountains of mashed potatoes steam swirling up high and the platter of brown-sugar–candied carrots, next to the basket of warm-from-the-oven rolls, just beggin' to be slathered with butter. *Oh, please, God, make this quick, amen.*

Dad says, "Dear Lord, I thank you for blessing our home and our work. We pray for the soul of Mrs. Diane Jeffers and for the comfort of the whole Jeffers family. We will work hard to serve their family to the best of our abilities and make us worthy of your great faith in us, oh Lord."

I think of Bub Jeffers. No way am I serving him.

Lizbreath passes, Mom talks, Nanbull talks, I pass, but in my head I say, *I'm grateful I helped Dad get the Jeffers call.*

Aunt Aggie says she's working on "mouse 999."

Chick goes last. "Thank you for dead leaves."

After dinner, Mom empties the blessing bowl into the garbage with the scrappy, cold clumps of beef fat and potato mush without ever reading the cards.

"A person's prayers are private," Mom says. "Besides, God's got big ears. God hears what's in your heart."

When the dishes are done, we sit in the living room. Dad turns on the Red Sox game and soon he's asleep on the couch. Aunt Ag falls asleep on the La-Z-Boy and soon she's honk-snoring too. Uncle Marty and Aunt Sal come over for coffee. Mom takes her favorite game, Pictionary, off the shelf and we play a few rounds. Lizbreath's on my team. Dad wakes up and watches us play. He says he's got three instant lottery tickets in his pocket for the winning team. Lizbreath and Uncle Marty are the last to draw. Lizbreath draws "racetrack" so well I get it right away. Our team wins. Lizbreath's a pain, but I'll give her one thing. That girl can draw.

We scratch off the tickets. No winners.

Dad turns on the football game. The Red Sox are one game shy of the series and now in football the Patriots are off to a roaring start. Can't ask for a better fall in the great old state of Massachusetts.

Aunt Aggie wakes up laughing.

"What's so funny?" Nanbull asks, and we all turn to listen.

"Make sure they take my hearing aid out," Aunt Ag says.

"What?" Nanbull says.

"When I go," Aunt Ag says, adjusting the little button in her ear. "Remember that story you told us, Sally?" Aunt Ag says, turning to look at Aunt Sally. "About how you were down in the prep room doing Mrs. Casey's hair and she started humming?"

Aunt Sal, Uncle Marty, Mom, Dad, and Nanbull all crack up laughing.

"What are you talking about?" I say.

"Your Uncle Marty was embalming Mrs. Casey," Aunt Sally explains. "Remember her? Sweet old lady, lived over on Forbes Avenue. Anyway, Uncle Marty had taken Mrs. Casey's hearing aid out and set it on her chest, then the phone rang and he got called away. He covered Mrs. Casey up with a sheet." Aunt Sally smiles.

"Then I came along to do Mrs. Casey's hair," Aunt Sally says. "It was back when I still used those metal rollers, now I use a curling iron, but anyway, I started working on Mrs. Casey's hair, when all of a sudden she starts humming."

"*What*?" I say.

"You mean she was still alive?" Lizbreath says, all spooked.

Chick giggles and claps her hands.

"Scared the livin' daylights right out of me," Aunt Sally says. "I was a hairdresser before this line of work and I was still a little shaky downstairs in the prep room alone. My girlfriends at the shop would joke with me and say, "Did you ever see one sit up, Sal?" And I'd say, "No, but the first one that does, is the last one I do.""

"But what about Mrs. Casey?" I ask.

"Well, I calmed myself down," Aunt Sally says.

"Figured my mind was playing tricks on me. I went to roll up another curler and sure enough Mrs. Casey starts humming again. I screamed and called for Uncle Marty and he came running." Aunt Sally starts laughing so hard she can't finish her story.

"What happened?" Lizbreath says.

Aunt Sally wipes her eyes. "Turns out the metal in the rollers was setting off the hearing aid."

"We had fun with that story for a long time," Dad says. "Good times." He shakes his head, smiling. "Hey, Sally, why was Mrs. Casey humming?"

"Because she didn't know the words."

Lizbreath sneers and rolls her eyes. "This family is so weird."

We play another round of Pictionary, then Mom makes roast beef sandwiches for supper. She warms up the apple pie for dessert.

Sundays are pretty good at my house.

Later, I lay in bed thinking how good it was to see my dad happy today for a change. How good it feels knowing that I was the one who got the Jeffers call for our family.

On Monday, all the good turns bad.

There's a rumor spreading around school.

Kip Campbell talks to dead people.

CHAPTER 8

Somebody's Shooting Cats

. . . man's reach should exceed his grasp;
or what's a heaven for?

—Robert Browning, 1812–1889

Mr. Jeffers must have told Bub that I heard his mother talking to me. And what if Mr. Jeffers broke down all guilty in the emotion of the moment and confessed how he's in love with his secretary, Liza, and that Bub's poor dead mother gave the green light for them to get married? And what if Mr. Jeffers told Bub the part I repeated from his mother about Bub being "hurt inside."

If Bub Jeffers hated me before, he's ready to kill me now.

Drew Callahan turns and walks the other way

when she sees me coming down the hall. I call her name, but she pretends she doesn't hear me.

Tia Moore doesn't give me Skittles in English.

Dirk Hogan shouts "freak" as I pass him in the cafeteria.

Zack Golden corners me. "So you Campbells want to play hardball, huh, making up lies about talking to the dead to trap families into giving you their business? What are you going to do next . . . hold séances? 'Ooh, lady, listen, did you hear that voice? It's your dead husband. He's saying to have the funeral here at Campbells. And, wait, listen, it's your dead great-granny too. . . .'"

"Shut up, Golden," I say. "It's not like that at all."

"Oh really, Campbell? My uncle says your father's running scared. Your business is collapsing. Your house is falling down. You can't compete with the big guns. Golden's is going to hammer you into the ground like a coffin, one nail at a time. You'll be six feet under by Christmas. Wait and see."

Tuck comes up to me, looking hurt. "What's Bub Jeffers spreading around about you talking to dead people?"

"Nothing," I say. "Bub's a liar." I'm not ready to

get into all of this with Tuck right now. I need to know why Drew is ignoring me.

After gym, Stew comes over, looking sort of scared, but intrigued. "Do you just *hear* voices, Kip, or do you actually *see* dead people too?"

I can't help myself. I look past Stew down the line of lockers. I widen my eyes to look spooked and point a shaky finger. "Stew, check it out! Do you see that? There's a ghost coming toward us right now!"

"*Where?*" Stew shouts, scrambling back, hitting his head against a locker, looking like he's gonna pee his pants.

"Just kidding, Stew," I say. "Settle down. You know me. I don't see ghosts."

"You're not funny, Kip," Stew says, walking away from me.

"Can't you take a joke?" I shout. "You know, *ghosts*. It's almost Halloween."

Jupe's the only one who doesn't seem to care. "So what," he says, shrugging his shoulders. "Cops call in people to help with cold cases all the time. My dad says these days everybody thinks they've got special powers."

Tuck stares at me at our lockers after school like I betrayed him or something.

"What?" I say.

"You tell me," Tuck says.

"*What?*" I say. "*What?*"

"Nothing," Tuck says. He slams his locker door and walks away.

I feel bad. I owe Tuck more than that. I owe him an explanation. He's my best friend. He's been my best friend since we were babies. We don't keep secrets from each other, especially a whale-size one like this.

At first I didn't tell Tuck about the voices because I didn't know how to explain it. Then I thought I was supposed to keep it a secret. I still haven't even told my parents. And I was almost done with the dead, until the gold deal. But I just can't help Bub Jeffers, not after all the mean stuff he's said to me my whole life. I'm so confused. "Hey, Tuck, wait . . ."

"Freak," Dirk says as he passes by me. "Deadbo, Flower Boy, *Freak*."

Drew Callahan comes up to me. She crosses her arms over her chest. "I thought you told me your father was selling the business. That he was opening a sports center. You do live in a funeral home. Bub was right. Why did you lie to me?"

"Your father's opening a sports center?" Stew says.

He's back getting something else out of his locker. "You never told us. . . ."

"Lay off me, Stew," I say.

I slam my locker, sling on my backpack, and walk home alone.

I e-mail Drew. She doesn't respond. I try again after dinner. I know she's online. She doesn't answer. The doorbell rings. Mom calls out. "Kip, Tucker's here."

Oh, good. I need to apologize.

Tuck looks all agitated. He motions for me to come outside.

"Somebody's shootin' cats!" he blurts out.

"*What*? What are you talking about?"

"Our next door neighbor, Mrs. Elkin, you know her, her cat Ju-Ju got shot with a BB gun yesterday," Tuck says. "Had to have surgery and everything. Cost Mrs. Elkin a thousand bucks."

"Wow," I say.

"And listen to this," Tuck says. "The vet told Mrs. Elkin it was the second cat that got brought in shot that day. And they were both black cats. The vet said close to Halloween you have to watch out. Crazy people do mean things to black cats."

"That's sick," I say, "who would do something like that?"

Then my body clenches cold. Mosely. *Where's Mosely?*

"Mosely . . . . Mosely." I walk around the house calling for my cat, making that puckered kissing sound that usually brings him running.

He doesn't come running.

I check every room, ask Mom and Dad, Chick and Lizbreath. Nanbull. Nobody's seen him all day.

Tuck and I search downstairs all through the funeral floor, the viewing room, parlor, office. No. I flick on the light and head downstairs. "Stay here," I tell Tuck. The prep room in the basement is locked. Mosely's not down here. I head back up. Shouldn't be outside either. Mosely is an indoor cat. If I take him out, I keep him on a leash. With the nature of our business, you can't have a cat roaming free as he pleases, bringing home prize mice during calling hours or jumping up in a coffin taking a catnap when he feels like it.

I get a sick feeling remembering something. When the Jeffers family was here for the arrangements session and Lizbreath went up to get coffee, she carelessly left the door open and Mosely snuck out and came downstairs into the parlor. Bub said, "What's that frigging cat doing here?" I wonder if Bub heard Lizbreath say, "It's Kip's cat."

Bub hates me. What if he's getting back at me through Mosely? Mom said Bub and Mr. Jeffers were here today dropping off some photographs for the memorial display board Mom puts together for the viewings.

"Come on, Tuck. We've got to find Mosely. Now."

First stop, Uncle Marty and Aunt Sally's. They've got three indoor cats, Winken, Blinken, and Nod. Those three lazy cats are the happiest cats in America. They've got a carpeted three-story cat hotel and a jungle gym, scratching posts in every room, fresh catnip-filled pillows and more toys then Cats R Us. Those cats are so flippin' happy they've never once tried to escape. Other cats keep hoping they'll get invited over. Sometimes Mosely leaps out our kitchen window over to Uncle Marty's porch to visit his cousins. It's quite a leap. I tell Mosely he's Super Cat when he does that. All he needs is a cat cape.

"No, Kip, sorry," Aunt Sally says when she answers the door. "Mosely hasn't been here all day."

Tuck and I check all around our property, including the garage. He's not in the hearse, Black Beauty, or Grandpa Campbell's antique hearse either. "Let's hit the neighbors," I say.

Tuck and I go up and down the street, checking every house in the neighborhood, knocking on doors, calling *Mosely! Mosely!*, me making that kissing sound, until it gets dark. I leave the outdoor lights on and a can of Mosely's favorite food by the front and back doors. Tuck has to go home.

"Sorry, Kip," he says. "Don't worry. He'll show up. Cats have nine lives, right?"

CHAPTER 9

The Golden Egg

Sincerity is the way of Heaven.

—Mencius, 372–289 B.C.

Tuck is waiting for me all out of breath the next morning at the corner. "Bub Jeffers is saying the Birdlady's kidnapping cats all over Clover."

"No way," I say.

Kids in Clover call Birdie O'Shaughnessy the Birdlady because her yard is filled with bird feeders and birdbaths and birdhouses and she's always got birds flocking around her when she's walking on the beach. Sometimes she even has a gull perched on her shoulder. So I guess she earned that nickname.

"Tia called me last night," Tuck says, all excited to be the one with the news. "She says Bub said the Birdlady is trapping cats in those yellow bags she's always collecting stuff in on the beach. After she kidnaps them she brings them back to her creepy cottage in the woods and then lets them loose so she can hunt them down. Who knows what she does with them then. Bub says she probably skins them and—"

"That's a lie!" I shout. "Birdie wouldn't do that."

"Birdie?" Tuck says. "The Birdlady's name is Birdie?"

"That's right. She's a friend of my grandmother's. I know her too. Birdie O'Shaughnessy's a little weird, but she would never hurt a cat. She wouldn't hurt a flea."

I think about how after I helped old Billy Blye move on to Good, his parrot, Hook, was down at Wayshak's Pet Store waiting for someone to adopt it. I figured Birdie would enjoy a pet, especially a bird, and so I claimed Hook, slung his cage on the handlebars of my bike, and delivered him to Birdie. She's never said so directly—Birdie's not much for small talk—but I know it made her happy.

When we get to school, Bub and Zack Golden are talking to Drew by the bike racks. They turn toward me. Drew is crying.

"What's wrong?" I say, moving close to Drew. They better not be teasing her.

"My cat's missing," Drew says, sniffling.

"I told her the Birdlady's stealing them," Bub says.

"She ain't no Birdlady," Zack says. "She's a witch."

"That's right," Bub says. "It's the witch that's doing it."

My heart's banging like house shutters before a nor'easter.

"Halloween's coming," Zack says. "Witches love cats." He stares straight into my eyes and smiles. "Especially black cats."

"Where's Mosely?" I say, moving up in his face, clenching my fists.

Zack laughs. "*Mosely*? Who's Mosely?"

"My cat. Where is he?"

"*Your* cat's missing too, Flower Boy?" Bub says, "Oh, boo hoo, that's sad."

"Shut up," I say, my head pounding. I swear if he didn't just lose his mother, I'd punch him flat out right here. What's he doing in school, anyway? Shouldn't he be home grieving with his dad and Maj?

"The witch stole your cat too?" Drew says to me, wiping her nose.

"She's not a witch and Birdie didn't steal anything," I say.

"*Birdie*?" Zack says, making a snorting sound. "The witch's name is *Birdie*?"

"Birdie O'Shaughnessy," I say. "And she's not a witch."

"Who is she then, Flower Boy, your *girlfriend*?" Dirk Hogan says, finally getting in on the action. Ever since Zack Golden arrived in Clover, Zack and Bub have been hanging tight. Dirk's the odd guy out. Dirk can see the graffiti on the wall. Zack's taking over his spot as Bub's best friend.

"Birdie and Flower Boy, sittin' in the tree," Dirk sings stupidly, "k-i-s-s-i-n-g."

Drew scowls at him like *grow up*. Nobody laughs. Dirk stops singing. I swear that kid's still stuck in second grade, probably still likes Captain Underpants.

"Drew, listen," I say, turning my backs on the jerks and lowering my voice so only she can hear. "I'll help you look for your cat after school if you want."

Drew purses her lips and cocks her head like she's thinking about it, like she's going to make me suffer for having lied to her until she's good and ready to give in.

"Okay," she says, sniffling. "Meet me at the pier at four."

Drew and her father live in a small gray clapboard Cape. No wreath on the plain blue door, no fall flowers in pots out front. Drew's mother is dead. I'm not sure what happened to her. Drew doesn't have any brothers or sisters. "It's just me and my dad and Pumpkin," she says. "I named her that 'cause she's orange."

I smile. "That's cute."

"Pumpkin's old and fat," Drew says. "She's always been a big eater. We tried putting her on a diet once, but she didn't like that at all. She kept following us around purring and when we didn't pay attention, she tore a hole in the bottom of a humongous new bag of cat food and it emptied out all over the floor. What a mess. It was a jackpot for Pumpkin, but I had to sweep it all up."

We knock on doors and look up in trees, calling Pumpkin's name. We reach the last house. No luck. We keep walking toward the water. When we reach the shore, Birdie O'Shaughnessy is trudging up the stairs in her rain slicker with a yellow plastic PriceCheck bag in each hand.

When she sees us, she sucks her head into her hood like a turtle. She passes us, smelling like smoke, and hurries off.

"Birdie," I say. "Wait. I want you to meet my friend."

Birdie keeps on walking. Birdie's not what you'd call a social butterfly. It took a lot to get her to talk to me the first time. She likes me okay now, but she's shy around new people.

Drew clenches my arm. "That's her?" she whispers. "The Birdlady?" Drew's eyes are bugging out scared. "Look, she's got those yellow bags like Bub said. What if she's got cats in there?"

"Cats don't hang out at the beach," I say. "Besides, I told you. I know Birdie. She's a woodle, but she's not evil."

The wind blows. Drew shivers. "It's cold," she says, zipping her jacket.

"Want to go?" I say.

"No," she says, starting down the stairs. "Let's walk a little." I follow her.

The beach is empty. I pick up a rock and toss it in the water. Drew stoops to pick up a shell. "Look," she says, coming up close to me. "Isn't it pretty?"

"Yeh, nice," I say, thinking about how nice she smells, how pretty she is.

Drew picks up a piece of green beach glass, rubs off the sand, holds it up to the light, and sticks it in her pocket.

"So how do you like Clover?" I say.

"It's all right, I guess. Better than the last place we lived. So boring. There weren't many kids my age and there wasn't much to do. I did have a best friend there, though. Chandler. That was the hardest part, leaving her. We talk every day online, but it's not the same as biking two streets down and walking right in her front door without even knocking because I'm one of the family."

I think that's the way it is with me and Tuck. I still owe him an explanation.

"I'm sorry," I say. "That's rough."

"So what's it like living in a funeral home?" Drew says, changing the subject.

"Nice," I say. "Everybody's just dying to come over."

Drew laughs and I laugh too.

"It's not true," I blurt out, "what I told you before about my dad buying a sports center." I pick up another rock and toss it into the water, scaring a few seagulls.

"I know," Drew says. "It's okay. I figured that out

a while ago. But explain to me what Bub's saying about you talking to dead people?" She scrunches up her shoulders and makes like she's shivering. "That's creepy, Kip."

I pick up a fat pink-and-red speckled crab, pincered legs kicking in the air, and toss it back into the water before a seagull can eat it. "Don't listen to Bub," I say. "That dude hates me. He always has. I don't know why."

"Wait," Drew says, stopping. "I need to run up to the restroom. I'll be right back."

"Sure," I say. "I'll wait here." I watch Drew run off and up the stairs, her brown hair floating up around her in the wind like angel wings.

There's a big old piece of driftwood. I sit down and look out at the water. The sun is low in the autumn sky. It casts a gold light on the beach. I watch a small white bird with black markings dive into the water for food. A gray gull caws. I turn and look up the beach. Something sparkly in the sand. I go to check it out.

It's a good-size rock, shaped sort of like an egg.

Except it's not a rock or an egg.

It's gold.

I pick it up. *Wow*. This thing must weigh a pound.

If those little nuggets I found after I helped Billy Blye—they weighed a couple ounces—were worth six hundred bucks, this thing, if it's real . . . I look up and down the beach. No one's around. I put the golden egg in my jacket and zip the pocket.

CHAPTER 10

Drew's Hero

The blessed damozel leaned out
From the gold bar of Heaven . . .

—Dante Gabriel Rossetti, 1828–1882

We head back to Drew's house, stopping at a few more places, calling "Pumpkin, Pumpkin!" but no luck. I look at Drew's pretty face, all sad and hopeless.

"I've got to go home now," I say, "but I'll help you put flyers around town tomorrow after school if you want. I need to make some up for Mosely, too." I feel a twist in my gut just thinking about what Bub Jeffers might have done with my cat.

As soon as I leave Drew's doorstep, I hightail it back to the beach, the golden egg burning a hole in my pocket. It will be dark soon, but I don't care. I've got questions for Birdie O'Shaughnessy. She was walking on the beach right before Drew and I came. Maybe she knows something.

The lights are on in Birdie's cottage, a swirl of smoke rising up from the chimney. Near the door, I hear Birdie talking. Maybe she has company. Then I hear Hook squawk. Birdie never has company. Birdie's just talking to her bird.

When I knock, the talking stops. Birdie will pretend nobody's home, but I know the drill by now. I knock again. "Birdie, it's me, Kip. Kip Campbell."

"I know yer last name, Skipper," Birdie says, unlatching the first lock and then the second, then opening the door. Her gray hair is all straggly around her face. She could sure use a haircut and a new set of teeth. Her eyes are pretty, though, like two blue robin's eggs.

Birdie peers over my right shoulder, then the left, nervously. "See any vandals around me property?"

"No, why?" I turn and look around the yard.

Meow. Meow. Mosely runs toward me from inside Birdie's cottage and before I can catch him he's out the door. "Mosely!" I shout. "What the heck?" Then another cat, a fat orange cat with a chocolate brown collar, bolts out over my feet, nearly tripping me, and takes off chasing Mosely.

I look at Birdie. "What's going on here?"

"What d'ya mean?"

"That's my cat, Mosely, and my friend Drew's cat, Pumpkin. What are you doing with our cats?"

"That's the mystery," Birdie says, shaking her head. She pulls a stubby cigarette out of her sweater pocket and lights it. She takes a puff and lets it out. I move out of the direction of the smoke.

"Moses and Pumpkin, huh?" Birdie smiles. "Them's nice names. But something's not right. Somebody's leaving cats on me doorstep. Two, three nights ago I heard noises outside. Wasn't sure if was the rain or the wind. I was too scared to check. The next morning, I go outside to fill the feeders and I nearly trip over this poor black cat lying on my porch. It was all wet and sickly looking. I brought it in by the fire to warm it up, put out a bowl of milk, but it just laid there. So I put it in a bag and brought him over to the animal hospital. They weren't open yet, so I left the cat there. I figgered they'd take good care of it."

"That must have been Mrs. Elkin's cat," I say. "The vet said that cat was shot."

"*Shot?*" Birdie says. "Oh, that's tragic. Poor little bit of a creature."

"You did the right thing, Birdie. The vet fixed that cat up fine."

I hear rustling in the leaves and turn to see Mosely and Pumpkin running back toward us. Mosely rubs against my leg and I pick him up and hug him tight. "Come here, Mose. I missed you." I scratch his head and all around his ears and hold him up in the air so I can look right into his big green eyes. "Don't you run away again. Do you hear me?"

"Come in, all a' ya, and warm up," Birdie says.

I walk in and Pumpkin follows. I close the door to keep the cats in.

"I don't think your Moses ran away," Birdie says, "or the Pumpkin-eater either."

"What do you mean?" I say, smiling. Moses, I like that.

"I think someone's stealing 'em, Skipper. Yesterday morning, there was a banging on me door. I got me frying pan and opened the door and there was a yellow bag with something squirming around inside all crazy to get out. A paw ripped through the plastic and I helped rip the rest and your Moses ran into me house. He's a nice cat you've got there, Skipper. He had fun teasing Hook and jumping up trying to reach me birds."

We look up at the paper cranes hanging on string from the rafters. Birdie makes one in honor of each person who dies in Clover. She comes to all the wakes at Campbell and Sons, whether she knew the deceased or not, takes a memorial card, kneels by the coffin to pay her respects, takes a whiff or two of the flowers, and then hightails it out of there before Lizbreath gives her grief. There must be a hundred cranes up there. I wave my hands in the air and it sets them all dancing.

"Then it happened again last night," Birdie says, lighting a crumple of newspaper under the logs in her fireplace. "Banging on my door. I get me frying pan again and unlock the top lock, keepin' the chain on, and sure enough, there's another yellow bag squirming and squealing and scratching on my doorstep. I bring it in and help it out of the bag. It's Peter Pumpkin-Eater. Your cat, Moses, he hides under the table when he sees her."

"Pumpkin. That's my friend Drew's cat."

"Heh," Birdie laughs. "Pumpkin's an eater all right. I scooped out a bit of tuna for each of them on plates. Pumpkin gobbled hers down, licked the plate clean, and then went after Moses's plate. Moses objected and Pumpkin hissed and Moses went off scaredy cat under the table." Birdie bursts out laughing. She lights another cigarette.

"Mosely's a peaceful guy," I say, defending my cat, hugging him close, kissing his head. "He doesn't like confrontation."

Birdie laughs and pokes a log with an iron stick. "Want some cocoa?" she says.

"No thanks, Birdie. I'm late for dinner. But thanks for taking care of the cats. I better get them home before it gets too dark." I think about Bub Jeffers and Zack Golden. It had to be them. "You should report this to the police, Birdie."

"No!" she says, her eyes bugging out all scared. "Nothing but trouble."

"But Birdie. There are these two kids, real mean jerks, at my school and they're accusing you of cat-napping."

Birdie bursts out laughing, showing all her bad teeth. "Nothing wrong with catnapping. A little snooze here and there."

"No, Birdie. They are spreading bad rumors that you are stealing people's cats and shooting them too."

Birdie waves her hands in the air, like she's shooing away mosquitoes. "Clover kids have been spreading stories about Birdie O'Shaughnessy forever. Since I was your age, you and that pretty girl I seen ya with on the beach. I don't care what people say. I know who I am. Any lies they tell are sins on their souls. Black marks they'll have to pay for some day."

Pumpkin is purring at the door. How am I going to get the cats home without a carrier? "Hey Birdie, any chance I could borrow Hook's cage to get the cats home safely and I'll bring it right back first thing tomorrow?"

"Sure, Skipper. That'd be fine. Hook's door is always open. He flies around free in here all the time. Don't like seeing him in a cage anyway. Ain't natural for a bird."

I coax Pumpkin into the cage and then nudge Mose in behind her and close it. Birdie walks outside with us. I think I see someone standing by that pine tree, but no, it's just a bush. A strong gust of wind blows through the yard, making all the bird feeders rattle and swing.

"Zip that coat, Skipper," Birdie says as she's closing her door, "or you'll catch yer death a' cold."

I hear laughing, and turn to look around the yard. I think I see an elbow sticking out from behind that shed. "Who's there?" I shout. I hear leaves rustling, the tall trees casting dark shadows from the woods. Mosely and Pumpkin shift position in the cage. It's cramped quarters in there. Pumpkin reaches out an orange paw and I shake it. She's probably scared to death thinking she's being kidnapped again. "It's okay, girl. Don't worry. Mose and I'll get you home safe to Drew."

When I knock on the blue door, Drew opens it and bursts out crying. "Pumpkin!" she shouts. "Oh, Pumpkin, I missed you! Where have you been?" Drew scoops the big orange ball of fur out of the birdcage and squeezes her tight. "Pumpkin, Pumpkin. Oh, thank you, Kip." With her free arm, Drew hugs me like I'm a hero. She brushes a lock of hair away from my eyes, then kisses me on the cheek. It all happens so fast I'm not sure it happened. I never got kissed before.

It starts raining as Mosely and I bike away. When I get home I run up to my room and lock the door. I look at the hero with the rock-star hair all wet from the daring cat rescue. I lean into the mirror, studying the spot where she kissed me. My face doesn't look any different, but Kip Campbell's a new man.

When I take off my jacket, I remember the golden egg. I was going to ask Birdie about it. I take it out and rub my hand over it. I wonder what it's worth? Probably a lot. Those couple of tiny nuggets I found on the beach after Billy Blye's funeral . . . they were worth six hundred and change each, enough to buy me and Tucker a spot at Camp Russell next summer.

I open my backpack and zip the golden egg into one of the inner pockets. I'll ask Birdie about it tomorrow when I bring Hook's cage back to her, then I'll bring it down to the Clover Stamp and Coin and ask the owner what it's worth.

It's late when I finish my homework. When I shut off the light, Mosely purrs contentedly. He leaps up on my bed and finds a warm spot by my feet. "Night, Mose."

I fall asleep smiling, thinking about Drew.

CHAPTER 11

Like a Tattoo

So instead of getting to Heaven, at last—
I'm going all along.

—Emily Dickinson, 1830–1886

I wake up smiling, still thinking about Drew. I take a long, hot shower, dry my hair, and put on boxers, a clean white tee, my favorite brown shirt, and my longest jeans. Then I reach for the bottle of cologne I bought at Abercrombie & Fitch with my Christmas money last year. The bottle is way back in my top drawer. I slap some on my neck and stash it back in the far corner. Don't want Lizbreath snooping around and finding it. My hand brushes against something hard. I pull it out. It's that gold four-leaf clover I found in the old blue trunk the day we discovered Guts. I'd forgotten all about it.

Tuck, Jupe, and Stewie had biked back into town

to get some furniture and food, and I was alone. I opened up the trunk, figuring it must have belonged to Johnny Abel, the old caretaker who died a few years back. He was Willow Grove Cemetery's Outdoor Guy. The town hired a landscaping company after Johnny died. I stick the clover in my pocket with the egg. Maybe it's real gold too.

Dad is waiting for me at the breakfast table with a flashy colored brochure. The National Funeral Directors' Association annual convention is in Las Vegas next week and would I like to go with him. "It's beautiful out there this time of year, Kip," he says. "We could see some shows, whatever you'd like."

"But Halloween's next week." I'm not thinking about candy. I'm thinking about Drew. I'm also thinking it's sort of creepy to be having a funeral director's convention on Halloween, but I don't say anything.

"Oh," Dad says, disappointed. "I thought maybe you were getting too old for trick-or-treating."

"No, Dad. I figure I've got another year or two."

"Okay, sure," Dad says.

I feel bad letting Dad down, but no way am I missing out on my date with Drew.

Lizbreath comes in wearing a long purple top with three rows of beaded necklaces, funeral jewelry probably. "What are you all dressed up for?" she says, studying me.

"I'm not," I say.

"Since when do you shower and blow-dry your hair in the morning?" she says.

I pour some juice, ignoring her.

Lizbreath comes up right next to my face and sniffs by my ears. I can smell her nasty morning breath. "Get away from me, Lizard," I say.

"You're wearing cologne!" she says as if she's made an important scientific discovery that will save the planet from imminent destruction.

Mom and Dad look at each other and smile. Oh, great. Can't a guy get a break? I pull the sports section over in front of me and make believe I'm reading.

Lizbreath can't let it go though. She's staring at me like a hawk in a tree waiting to pounce on a mouse.

"*What*?" I say. "What's your problem?"

"Kip," Mom says, "if you can wait five minutes, I've got apple spice muffins in the oven."

"Thanks, Mom, but I'm good with cereal." I dump a hill of Frosted Flakes into a bowl. "Pass me the milk, will you, Liz?"

Lizbreath slides the carton my way, still staring at me. My cheeks redden like she can read my mind or something.

Please tell Bub it's not his fault. Mrs. Jeffers's voice jolts me and I jump.

"What?" Lizbreath says, squinting at me.

I can't go until you tell him, Mrs. Jeffers says, her voice booming like the bells at St. Mary's. My ears sizzle. I can't believe my whole family doesn't hear her. I look quickly around the kitchen. Mom pours a cup of coffee. Dad flips to a new section of the newspaper. Chick pops her head up from underneath the table and says, "Boo!"

"Ahh!" I shout, truly spooked.

Chick giggles hysterically. "I got you, Kip," she says. "I got you good!"

When I head out for school, Mom says, "Please yell down to Uncle Marty that there's fresh coffee and muffins. He's been working since the crack of dawn."

I walk downstairs, past the Christophers, then one more flight down to the prep room. The lights are all on. The door is open. Uncle Marty is standing at the table wearing a surgical smock, working on

Mrs. Jeffers's body. When he hears me, he nods and smiles. "Morning, Kip." He pulls a white sheet up over Mrs. Jeffers out of respect.

If I was ever going to be a funeral director, which I'm not, the one thing burned into my brain like a tattoo about this profession is the word "respect."

R-E-S-P-E-C-T.

My Dad and Uncle Marty do every single thing they do with respect. One memory stays etched in my mind. I was mad because my father missed a Little League game. Our team had made the state finals. One more win and we were going to Orlando—Orlando, FLORIDA!!—for the nationals. When I got up to bat, I looked up in the stands for the spot where the Campbells always sit. The Campbells are big into baseball. We've got Red Sox all-American baseball blood coursing through our veins . . . and there were Mom and Liz and Nanbull and Aunt Aggie and Uncle Marty and Aunt Sally, but no Dad. I tried to shake it off, but I couldn't. *Strike one. Strike two.* Come on, Dad, where are you? *Strike three. Yer . . . OUT!*

That night I was so mad, I nearly spit in his face when he finally came upstairs. "I'm sorry, Kip," he said. "I wanted so much to be there. But right when

I was leaving to come, I got a call that Mrs. Delaney had died."

"I don't care about some old dead lady!" I said. "She's *dead*, Dad. She could have waited an hour. Where the heck's she gonna go?"

"But Kip—"

"But nothing, Dad."

My father left me alone. He came back after dinner, knocked on my door.

"Come with me, son. I want to show you something."

Dad brought me down into the prep room in the basement, usually off-limits to me and Liz. There was a body on the table. Dad lowered the sheet just enough so that I could see the face.

"That's Mrs. Corrine Delaney," Dad said. "I've known her since I was your age. I delivered papers to her every morning when I was a boy and she tipped me better than anybody else in Clover. Gave me a twenty dollar bonus one Christmas. Twenty dollars was like a million bucks back then. I went to school with her daughter, Marcia. I had such a crush on that girl. Took her to the junior prom, then she dumped me for Frankie Sorrentino. Married him and moved out to Arizona, haven't heard from her in twenty years.

"Then Marcia called me this morning, crying, saying could I come to the hospice. Her mother just died. 'You remember my mother, don't you, Chris?' she said to me when I got there. I said, 'Sure I do, Marcia.' I told her about that Christmas bonus. Marcia started crying. 'That was my mother,' she said. 'Always doing nice things for people.' We shared more stories about her mother. She introduced me to her children, Janice and Charlie."

"Yeah, whatever," I said.

"I'm sorry, Kip," my dad said, his eyes filling with tears. "God knows I wanted to be at your game. I'm so proud of you, son. I love watching you play. But I had to answer that call, Kip. I am a funeral director. We are Campbell and Sons Funeral Home. That's my job. Just like Doc Burton has to jump up and go, morning, noon, or night, when a new baby's ready to come in to Clover. I'm there for our neighbors on the other end of life, morning, noon, or night."

I looked down at Mrs. Delaney's face.

"This isn't just some dead body, Kip," my dad said. "This is Richard's wife, and Marcia's mother, and Janice and Charlie's grandmother. That's what we have to remember, son."

Tell Bub it's not his fault, Mrs. Jeffers's voice booms over my memories like a gong, jarring me back to the present.

"Hey, Uncle Marty," I say, "Mom said to tell you to come up for breakfast. She's got muffins coming out of the oven."

"Sounds good," Uncle Marty says. "I'm hungry. Thanks, Kip." He takes off his gloves, hangs up his smock, turns on the faucet, and scrubs his hands. "Did you find Mosely yet?"

"Yeah, thanks."

Kip, Mrs. Jeffers says in an urgent voice, *tell Bub that little bit of watermelon didn't matter. I was going to die that night anyway.*

What? What watermelon?

"Kip?" Uncle Marty is staring at me from the doorway with a quizzical expression on his face. "Are you all right?"

"Oh yeah, sure, sorry." I walk out first. Uncle Marty shuts off the light and locks the door.

"Have a good one, Uncle Marty." I run up the stairs, past the Christophers, and outside. The cool, fresh air feels good. I can't wait to see Drew at school. I won't ever tell her about hearing dead people. She said she thought that was creepy.

Please, Kip, tell Bub . . .

"No!" I shout, putting my hands over my ears. "I'm sorry, Mrs. Jeffers, but I'm done. I don't want to be a freak!"

CHAPTER 12

Bull's-Eye

I was a child and she was a child,
In this kingdom by the sea,
But we loved with a love that was more than love—
I and my Annabel Lee—
With a love that the winged seraphs of Heaven
Coveted her and me.

—Edgar Allan Poe, 1809–1849

I'm sure it was either Bub Jeffers or Zack Golden or maybe both of them who kidnapped Mosely and Pumpkin and shot Mrs. Elkins's cat and scared poor Birdie even further into her turtle shell.

One of them is going to pay.

I tell Tuck what I found out about the missing cats. He says he'll help me investigate after school. Stew has to work at the diner with his mom and I decided not to involve Jupe. Jupey will want to talk to his dad and there's no sense getting the police involved. I want to get even myself.

There's a long, winding driveway up to the Jeffers' house. Mr. Jeffers owns a whole chain of Jiffyspray car wash businesses. As Lizbreath says, they're loaded.

It's a huge white house with tall columns and a fancy carved door and shrubs shaved into perfect shapes, and loopy trees that don't look natural in Massachusetts.

I go straight to the door and ring the bell, no sneaking around like a sissycat. I'm not afraid of Bub Jeffers. He's going to pay for what he did. Tuck is right beside me.

Bub's sister, Majestic, answers the door. "Bub's out back in the yard." She looks down at our shoes. "I'll let you come through the house if you take off your shoes."

"No, that's okay," I say. "We'll walk around."

"Suit yourself," she says. "I'll unlock the side gate." She taps a button on a security box. "See ya."

Tuck and I open the gate and walk around behind the house.

There's Bub. His back is to us. He's holding a rifle, maybe it's a BB gun, in his hand and he's aiming at a clay pigeon sitting across the yard on a fence.

"What the—" Tuck whispers.

I motion to Tuck to be quiet. I don't want to startle Bub with a gun in his hand.

Pow! Bub lets the trigger go. The bullet hits the bird, and pieces of clay spray everywhere.

"Bulls-eye!" Bub shouts, cocking his elbow into his side in a victory pose. "Oh yeah. Who's the man?" He laughs and sets the gun down.

"Some man," I say.

Bub swings around. "What are you doing here?" He reaches for the gun.

"Don't touch that," I say. "One call to Jupe's father about you aiming a gun at us and you'll be in Mass juvie court quicker than you can say trick or treat on Halloween."

"That's right," Tuck says.

"What do you want, Campbell?" Bub says, looking past us, around the yard, like he's wondering if Stew and Jupe are here too. Stew's no threat, but Jupe's another matter. Jupe doesn't like fighting, but if he had to, he'd cream ya.

"Did you shoot Mrs. Elkin's cat?" I say.

Bub snickers. *"What?* No way."

"You kidnapped my cat, though, right? And Drew's?"

"You're sick, Campbell," Bub says, shaking his head disgustedly. "Why the heck would I care about chasing cats? I've got better things to do."

"Yeah, like what?" Tuck says. "Shooting fake birds?"

"Shut up, Stucker," Bub says.

"No. You shut up!" I shout. "Mrs. Elkin's cat was shot with a BB gun just like the one you've got there and then somebody dumped it on poor Birdie O'Shaughnessy's porch. You shot the cat, didn't you? Come on, admit it. And then you kidnapped my cat, Mosely, and Drew's cat too."

"What's going on here?" a loud voice demands.

I turn around. Mr. Jeffers is standing there with an angry look on his face. I was shouting so loudly at Bub that I didn't hear him come up behind us.

"What's this about you shooting a cat?" Mr. Jeffers says to Bub, his face all red.

"I don't know, Dad," Bub says, looking nervous. "Campbell's making up some whacked-out lie."

"I warned you, Bradley, about . . ." Mr. Jeffers moves toward his son.

Bub's name is Bradley. Who knew?

"No, Dad, I swear," Bub pleads, sounding scared. He backs away from his father.

Tuck and I look at each other.

"That's it, Bradley, you're done," Mr. Jeffers says, picking up the gun, all red-faced and furious. He cracks it open, dumps out the bullets. "See you later, boys," he says to me and Tuck, nodding his head like *get out of here, now.*

As Tuck and I make our way back out front we hear Mr. Jeffers shouting. "What the heck's wrong with you? Didn't you learn your lesson the last time?"

There's a smacking sound and a crash.

"Dad, please!" Bub's shrieking. "I swear it wasn't me."

Tucker looks at me like maybe he feels a little sorry for Bub. I know what Tuck's thinking. Tuck's father has a wicked temper too. Tuck's father hits him too.

We bike down the driveway in silence. I feel all twisted and sick inside, more confused than ever. What if Bub didn't do it? What if it was Zack Golden?

Now you've made matters worse. Mrs. Jeffers is crying in my ears. *Please, Kip . . .*

"Shut up!" I scream. "Just shut up!"

"Whoa." Tuck slams on his brakes.

I stop too.

"What's wrong with you, Kip?" Tuck says.

I stare at my best friend, my stomach gurgling up, ready to puke. I want to tell him, tell him everything, but I can't. It's just too much. He won't understand.

"Nothing," I say.

"Why'd you tell me to shut up?"

"Sorry, Tuck," I say. "Just leave me alone, all right? I've got a lot on my mind."

Tuck looks at me for a long time. He nudges his broken glasses back up on his nose. "Is this about the million dollars?" he says.

"What?"

"Don't you remember? You told me if we found out what happened to Billy Blye it was worth a million bucks."

Please, Kip, talk to Bud. Tell him he didn't do anything wrong.

Stop! I scream inside. I don't want all this pressure. Keep your gold. I don't want it. I feel like I'm gonna start bawling. "I gotta go, Tuck. I'll call you later."

I bike home fast, run upstairs, head straight to my room so I don't have to talk.

"Kip, wait," Dad says.

"Hold on, Kip," Mom says. "We need to speak with you."

"Be there in a minute," I say. I need some time to think. Alone.

I walk in my room. *What!?*

There's a guy sitting at my desk. At my computer. Two duffel bags on the floor. The foldaway bed all made up with a yellow quilt and pillows.

The guy looks at me and nods his head. "Hello."

"Who are you?" I say.

"Kip, honey," Mom says, coming up behind me with Dad.

"I'm sorry," Dad says. "You didn't give us a chance to explain. This is Jason Landon. Jason, this is our son, Christopher. Jason is in the funeral service program at Mount Ida, Kip. He's going to be interning with us till Christmas."

CHAPTER 13

Lizard in Love

By heaven, I do love,
and it hath taught me to rime,
and to be melancholy.

—William Shakespeare, 1564–1616

"Sorry about the inconvenience," Jason, the funeral director intern, says. "I'll try to stay out of your way."

"That's all right," I say.

It would have been nice to have some warning, but it's not Jason's fault. Dad's been talking about getting a new intern for a while now. I've had to share my room before.

Jason says when he gets his license, he'll be a third-generation funeral director. His family ran a funeral home on Cape Cod until the Golden Corporation rode into town and put them under.

"We couldn't compete with their prices," Jason says. "They buy everything in bulk—the coffins, the vaults, equipment, chemicals, cars—and they do all their embalming at a central shop serving seven or eight funeral homes in a pod. They've got embalmers working for a flat fee, moving bodies in and out like an assembly line. In one year they bought us, Clinton's, Chicorelli's, and Bocketti's, sold off the buildings, but kept our names for the goodwill factor. Landon-Clinton-Chicorelli-Bocketti, that's a mouthful, huh? They figured people would be fooled into thinking they're locally owned and managed. The only funeral home still standing in Bramble is McNulty's."

My dad shakes his head. "I'm sorry, Jason. I knew your father for decades. He was a fine funeral director. One of the old guard. One of Massachusetts's best."

"Dad held off as long as he could," Jason says. "We'd owned that business for nearly a century. Our family lived upstairs. My dad was born in that house. My sister Emma and I grew up there. My grandfather and grandmother were waked there. It broke my dad's heart to sell out," Jason said. "He died of a heart attack two months later."

"I'm sorry, son," my father says, clapping his big bear palm on the intern's back. "I know your dad's proud of you, though, carrying on his legacy like this."

"Thank you," Jason says, nodding.

My father looks at me. I look the other way.

"Will you try to buy back the home when you get your license?" Dad asks.

"I can't afford it," Jason says. "The price of real estate on Cape Cod is crazy. Way out of my reach. And it's not even a funeral home anymore. I heard some lady runs a wedding-planning business there now. Imagine?" He shakes his head. "From funerals to weddings. Crazy."

"Dinner!" Mom calls to us and we head downstairs. We're having chili and corn bread.

Lizbreath comes in smelling like she took a bath in perfume. She has her hair all jazzed up and she's wearing a lacy blouse, blue eye shadow, and fancy funeral jewelry. She sits across from Jason and smiles at him. "Hi, again," she says.

"Hi," Jason says. He looks uncomfortable. He puts his napkin on his lap and takes a long drink of water.

We say grace and start eating. Lizbreath doesn't pick up her spoon. She's staring at Jason like a zombie in a trance. I dig in to the chili. "It's delicious, Mom."

"Hey, you," Chick says to Jason.

"Yes?" Jason says, brushing corn bread crumbs from his face.

"Lizzie says you're hot," Chick says, then bursts into giggles.

I laugh.

Lizbreath is in such a daze she doesn't even flinch.

So this is what it looks like. A lizard in love.

Good, at least she's off my case for a while.

I think about Drew, wondering what she's doing tonight.

Only five more days until our date. Trick or treat and maybe more kissing.

After dinner I head outside to rake leaves. Mrs. Jeffers's visitation is tomorrow. When I finish and come in, tired and cold, the phone is ringing. Mom answers it.

"It's for you, Kip," she says.

I pick up the receiver. "Hello."

"You're dead, Campbell," and then a click and a dial tone.

I recognize the voice. Bub Jeffers.

The doorbell rings. A florist making another late delivery of flowers for Mrs. Jeffers. Mom asks if I'll go down. I walk past the wall of Christophers. The viewing room is all set for tomorrow. All the chairs in neat rows. Floral sprays and baskets everywhere. Tomorrow, just before three, Uncle Marty and Dad will bring up Mrs. Jeffers in the pink casket delivered this afternoon, wearing the elegant funeral gown with the mink trim that was shipped special delivery overnight from Paris. Lizbreath begged to try it on, but Dad refused, of course. Aunt Ag will start the music. . . .

I toss and turn all night. I wake up shaking in a cold sweat. I picture Mrs. Jeffers in the prep room in the basement. She's sitting up on the table, crying. *Please, Kip, I beg you. Tell Bub that little bit of watermelon was the sweetest gift anyone gave me at the end. I was going to die that night anyway. It wasn't his fault. Not at all. Just God's plan. Please, Kip, be Bub's friend. Tell Bub how much I love him, always and forever. Please.*

CHAPTER 14

Breakfast at Nanbull's

Large was his bounty, and his soul sincere,
Heav'n did a recompense as largely send;
He gave to mis'ry all he had, a tear,
He gained from Heav'n ('twas all he whish'd)
a friend.

—Thomas Gray, 1716–1771

I wake up thinking about Mrs. Jeffers. What do I do? What do I do? No gold is worth this grief.

I get dressed and walk upstairs to Nanbull's. I'm fairly certain she's sitting alone at her kitchen table drinking a pot of tea. I knock quietly so as not to disturb Aunt Aggie.

"Kip," Nanbull says, her eyes lighting up. "Come in. I'll make you breakfast."

I'm too upset to eat, but I don't refuse. I know how happy it will make her to cook me a meal. In minutes, Nanbull places a steaming plate in front of me, scrambled eggs and sausage, hot cocoa, and cinnamon-swirl toast with butter.

Suddenly, I find my appetite. I push Mrs. Jeffers and the whole Jeffers family out of my mind, pick up a fork, and dig in.

I hear Aunt Aggie coughing in her room. "How's she doing?" I ask.

"Nights are the hardest," Nanbull says, "but she's hanging in there. She's almost finished knitting mouse one hundred."

Nanbull goes to the stove for the pan of hot chocolate, then refills my cup to the brim. "I'm so glad you came up, Kip. What a nice surprise. Remember how you used to come up nearly every morning when you were little?"

Nanbull sits facing me, smiling, taking great joy in watching me eat.

"I know. I remember," I say, sinking my teeth into the cinnamon-swirl toast. "This is great, Nanbull, thanks."

"My pleasure," she says.

Go to him now, Kip, Mrs. Jeffers shouts in my

ears, *before school starts. I'm afraid he might run off or something worse. His father can be so hard on him.*

"No!" I shout. My fork slams down on the plate.

Nanbull looks at me, startled, then her face softens kindly and she leans forward, clutching her wrinkled hand on my arm, locking my eyes in hers. "What's wrong, dear boy? Tell me."

And then *crack*, just like that, I'm crying. I didn't plan it, but I've been holding all of this in for so long that when the dam breaks it just all gushes out. Every bit of it. About the voices and how I've got this job helping the dead go to Good and how I tried giving it up because I need a real job that pays money so I can buy my Nauset Whaler and then Billy Blye died and I refused to get involved, but then I got offered this golden deal and that sounded good and I made enough money to pay for Tuck to go to Camp Russell with me next summer, our first time ever, and so I was thinking this job wasn't so bad after all, but then I heard Mrs. Jeffers talking to me right there in the parlor when the Jeffers family came to interview us and then Bub Jeffers stole the cats and I hate that kid, he's made fun of me my whole life, and now his mother wants me to be his friend, no way, I just can't . . .

"I see," Nanbull says, calmly, like this isn't a

surprise to her at all. She takes a sip of tea and puts it down. She hands me a napkin to wipe off my face.

I feel better.

"That explains why you asked to talk with Barry Jeffers privately during the arrangements session," Nanbull says.

"Yes," I say. "Mrs. Jeffers kept begging me to tell him something. And at first I said no, I hate Bub Jeffers, he's so mean to me, but then I thought, wait, maybe I can help Dad get the call and I know how much we need the money."

Nanbull tilts her head to the side and smiles. She reaches out to touch my arm. "You are so good, Kip. Such a big heart. I'm proud of you."

I stand up, walk to the sink. "I was proud to get the call for Dad," I say, my voice cracking. "I know we're in big trouble with Golden's taking our business. But then it spread all over school that I talk to dead people and kids are calling me a freak." I start to cry again. "And that Jeffers kid, he's got problems, he's got a gun, I got him in trouble with his father. He's out to get me big-time now."

"It's like I always say," Nanbull says. "The dead ones will never hurt you. It's the live ones you've got to watch out for."

Nanbull's trying to cheer me up, but I'm not in a joking mood.

"Kip," she says, standing up and coming toward me.

I look at her and start bawling like a baby. But so what, who cares? My grandmother's not going to tell anybody.

Nanbull takes my face in her hands. She wipes the tears off my face. I see the blue veins beneath the skin on her wrinkled hand, the thin gold wedding band.

"How can I help?" she says.

"I don't know, Nan. It's too confusing. *I don't want to be a freak.*" I turn away from her. "I hate this funeral stuff. Why can't we live in a normal house? Like a normal family. This business is a curse."

Nanbull looks like I slapped her. "This isn't a business," she says. "It's a calling. The work of saints and princes."

"I'm sorry, Nanbull, I didn't mean—"

"And you are not a freak, Christopher Gerald Campbell. You are my beautiful grandson. You are a prince of a boy. One of the lucky ones."

"*Lucky?* How?"

Please, Kip, go, before it's too late, Mrs. Jeffers's voice is booming in my ears.

Nanbull's staring at me. "You're hearing something, right?" she says.

I nod my head.

"What a gift," Nanbull says. She smiles at me, her blue eyes glistening with tears. She reaches out and touches my ear, her palm warm on my cheek.

"Go, Kip. Use your gift. Do what you're called to do."

CHAPTER 15

The Fisherman

Work is love made visible. And if you cannot
work with love but only with distaste,
it is better that you should leave your work
and sit at the gate of the temple
and take alms of those who work with joy.

—Kahlil Gibran, 1883–1931

It's early. Clover is quiet. I bike into town, past the gas station, Rubin's Auto, PriceCheck, Walgreen's, Sam's Sips and Subs, Belcher's bowling alley, Paulie's Pub, the Arcadia cinema, the Bumblebee Diner. Mrs. B is at the counter talking with a customer.

Down on the docks, Mr. Maloney and two of his workers are hauling the big boats up out of the water for the season. There's my Nauset Whaler, the biggest beauty of all. I watch the water drip off as she rises.

When they haul the tarp over her, she'll rest there

all winter like some giant sleeping ghost ship, hoping for a captain next spring. Someday it will be me.

I walk along the pier, smelling yesterday's gutted fish, gasoline from the motors. There's a fisherman in a Red Sox cap and windbreaker gearing up his boat for the day. He looks up at me and nods.

It's the guy I saw the morning after Billy Blye moved on. He said he was new in town, but he had already heard about my dad. The men here in Clover are tight. They hang out at the Elks Lodge on Saturday night. My dad is something of a local hero. He has buried at least one person every one of those men loved. A wife, a mother, a father, a brother. Dad knows their family stories, probably lots of family secrets, too. Comes with the territory.

"How's it going?" the fisherman says. He looks like he's in his twenties, about the age of Jason Landon. He's got green eyes, dark hair, and a scrappy beard. Lizbreath would probably have a crush on him, too. He dumps a bucket of bait in a cooler and throws a rope onto his rig.

"Good," I say. "How 'bout you?"

"I'll let you know around four o'clock," he says, laughing. "The thing about this line of work is, you never know if it's going to be your worst day ever or your best day ever. It all depends on the fish."

"Good luck," I say.

"You too, Kip," he says.

I turn around. "You have a good memory," I say. "You remembered my name from a couple of weeks ago?"

"Nah," he says, "I'm lucky if I remember where my traps are. Your dad, Chris Campbell, talks about you all the time down at the lodge. Always saying what a great kid you are and how proud he is."

"Oh," I say quietly.

My dad does that?

"That's a gift," the guy says.

"What is?"

"Having a father who loves you like that."

Biking away, I think about what the fisherman said about my dad bragging about me. Then I remember how Mr. Jeffers treated Bub when Tuck and I confronted him about the cats.

Please, Kip, now, I hear Mrs. Jeffers pleading.

I turn the corner and bike toward the Jeffers' house, fast before I change my mind.

Mr. Jeffers is pulling out of the driveway onto the street. Majestic is in the front seat. I don't see Bub. I wait until their car is out of sight, then I bike up the driveway and ring the bell. No one answers. I ring it again, holding the buzzer.

"Okay, okay, I'm coming!" I hear Bub shout. Then the door opens and we're facing each other.

"What do you want?" he says. Bub's wearing blue boxers, no shirt, an orange-and-yellow-polka-dotted towel around his neck, hair dripping wet.

He doesn't look so tough like this.

"I need to talk to you," I say.

He sneers at me like I'm Mosely turd. "You've done enough talking, Campbell." He shakes his head, flinging the water off. A drop lands on my cheek.

"Why'd you lie to my father about shooting that cat," he says. "I didn't do it."

"Really?" I'm not buying this.

"It was Zack Golden. That kid's psycho. He was over shooting pigeons with me and he took one of our BB guns home. We were both in on kidnapping your cat and that new girl, Drew's, but when you said Mrs. Elkin's cat got shot . . ." Bub shakes his head. "That was sick, man. I told him so. You better watch out for him, Flower Boy. Golden's got it in for you."

"Can I come in?" I say. "I have something to tell you. Something important."

Bub laughs. "Sure, Deadbo, come on in. Dad and

Maj just went to get donuts. When they get back, why don't we sit around the kitchen table and have a little party before we drive over to your house for my *mother's wake*. Wait, shouldn't you be home setting up flowers and all that other creepy stuff you weirdos do?"

My chest is pounding. My fists clench. All I want to do is punch him. I take a breath. *Just do it, Kip*. "Your mother wants me to tell you something."

"*Liar!*" Bub shouts and pushes me hard with both palms. My head cracks back against a column. He grabs me by the collar and pulls me toward him, then sucker punches me in the gut.

"Hey, no. Stop!"

"Come on, Flower Boy, fight!" Bub shouts, baring his teeth like a mongrel dog.

Tell him now, Kip, Mrs. Jeffers is pleading with me. *Please, tell him it wasn't his fault I choked. I was going to die that night anyway. . . .*

"Your mother said it wasn't your fault she choked. She was going to die that night anyway."

"*Shut up!*" Bub screams. "You're a friggin' freak! Get away from me, Flower—"

Please, Kip, tell him.

Bub Jeffers is screaming in my face. Mrs. Jeffers is screaming in my head.

I'm going to explode. I am a freak. I'm a freak. I'm a freak.

Please Kip tell him that little bit of watermelon was the sweetest, kindest thing anyone did for me at the end.

"Your mom says to tell you that the little bit of watermelon you fed her—"

"*How do you know about that?*" Bub shrieks, wild-eyed and terrified now.

Please tell him not to blame himself. I was going to die that night anyway.

"Your mother needs to know that you won't blame yourself for her death. She needs to know that you're okay before she can move on."

"*Stop!*" Bub shouts, his lips pursed tight and his whole face quivering like it's taking every ounce of strength in his body not to cry. He picks up a fat ceramic pot of red mums and slams it hard against the house. The pot cracks, dirt pouring down, scattering everywhere. He picks up the other pot and slams it down on the porch.

"Bub—"

"*No!*" he screams.

I step back.

Bub stands there facing his house, his back to me, body shaking, sobbing. I hear a car pulling up the driveway. Bub whimpers and sniffs.

"All they'd given her for weeks was friggin' gook in a tube, just waiting for her to . . ." He yelps like a dog caught in a trap, "just waiting for her to *die*."

I feel bad for him. I start crying too.

"There was a sign on her door—no food, not even water by mouth. They were covering their own butts. They were afraid she'd suck food into her lungs and get pneumonia and my father would sue them. Like he cared. He just wanted her gone."

Bub's crying hard now, not even trying to cover it. A car door opens and shuts, then another opens and shuts. Mr. Jeffers and Majestic.

Bub swings around, tears streaming down his face. "Do you know what it's like having your own mother laying there dying, begging you for a little food, a friggin' taste of watermelon? Do you? DO YOU, FLOWER BOY?"

"No," I say, my whole body shaking. "I'm sorry, man. I can't imagine that. You did the right thing, Bub. You were brave. Like your mom said, you giving her that little bit of watermelon was the sweetest, kindest thing anybody did for her at the end. She was grateful for it, Bub. She was on her way that night anyway. She's good now, Bub, knowing you're okay. Now she can move on."

I hear voices, then Mr. Jeffers and Majestic coming up the stairs behind me. Bub turns away quickly, wiping the orange and yellow towel over his face.

Tell him I love him, Kip, and his father does too. Shout it, Kip, just like that.

"Your mom says she loves you, Bub," I shout, "and your father does too."

I hear someone suck in air. I turn around. It's Mr. Jeffers.

His face is trembling like ocean waves.

I nod respectfully. "Sir." I head down the stairs. I get on my bike. I turn to look.

Mr. Jeffers and Bub are hugging like they're never going to stop.

Majestic is rubbing her brother's back.

CHAPTER 16

The Port of Heaven

I find the great thing in this world
is not so much where we stand, as it is in
what direction we are moving: To reach
the port of heaven, we must sail sometimes
with the wind and sometimes against it—
but we must sail, and not drift, nor lie at anchor.

—Oliver Wendell Holmes, 1809–1894

Leaving the Jeffers' house, I bike to school feeling lighter and freer and good. It's a short day. I have to leave early so I can go home and sweep those blasted leaves off the walkway and front steps before Mrs. Jeffers's first visitation at four o'clock.

Mom and Dad are at the kitchen table. Dad's hunched over a letter, clenched fists cradling his temples like he's reading very bad news.

When Dad sees me, he folds up the letter and stands.

"What, Dad? Tell me."

"It's not your concern, son."

"Yes it is," I say. "It's about the business, right? I want to know. Tell me."

Dad looks at Mom. She nods her head yes.

"It's a notice from the State of Massachusetts. We have thirty days to conform to code on ventilation and the new hazardous materials disposal regs or they'll close us down."

"Oh, Dad, I'm sorry."

"This isn't the first letter," he says. "They've been threatening us for a year." He nods to the potty-mouth jar on the counter. "And if we only had ten thousand dollars in that jar, I'd have fixed those problems a long time ago."

Nanbull would have to do an awful lot of swearing.

"Chris," Mom says, "there is nothing we can do about it at the moment." Mom looks at the clock. "This is Diane Jeffers's time."

A good crowd turns out for Mrs. Jeffers's first visitation and even more for the second one this evening. I'm out here in the parking lot, the Outdoor Guy, directing cars in an orderly fashion. I see Dad and Mom at the front door, greeting each guest with a handshake or hug as they arrive. Other funeral homes might pay someone to do that job, but not my family. Dad says it is important that someone from the Campbell family welcomes each guest to our home personally.

I can picture Lizbreath inside pointing out where the coat room and restroom are, all the time keeping her eyes on Jason Landon. Nanbull will be inviting people to sign the register book and take a memorial card. Aunt Ag's too sick to play the organ tonight so Mom selected a classical music tape. "Something comforting," she said.

I smile thinking about Chick skipping around asking, "Who wants a smiley-face sticker? You do? Good! Do you want red, yellow, green, or blue?"

Our whole class shows up to pay their respects, of course. It's Bub Jeffers, and not everybody likes him, but it's not every day somebody's mother dies. Mrs. O'Brien, our principal, comes, and every single teacher in our school.

Sal Mancuso shows up in a dapper suit. Sal owns Sal's Sips and Subs. He's got a crush on Nanbull. Sal keeps giving me free meatball subs and chocolate shakes, hoping I'll put in a good word for him. I'm stringing Sal along like a sleepy fish after bait. Gotta keep those subs coming my way.

Doc Burton arrives then Father Tallman with his old black-leather prayer book. "Hello, Kip."

"Hello, Father."

When Drew Callahan shows up looking so sad, I get Tuck to watch the parking lot for me, and I walk Drew inside my house.

"Thanks, Kip," she says nervously. She smells like tangerines. She's wearing a pretty black dress and high heels, her hair drawn back in a ponytail.

"No problem," I say.

When we enter the viewing room, I hear Drew make a whimpering sound and she claps her hands over her mouth.

I put my arm around her. "It's okay," I say.

"Funerals don't usually bother me," Drew says. "Bub was a jerk for kidnapping Pumpkin, but I know what it's like to lose your mother. I feel bad for him."

"I know," I say. "Me too."

I put my hand on the crook of Drew's elbow, like I've seen my dad do when he's escorting people, and I move Drew forward into the line of people waiting to pay their respects to Majestic, Bub, and Mr. Jeffers.

When I reach Bub, I stick out my hand. "I'm sorry for your loss, Bub."

He shakes my hand awkwardly. His palm is sweaty. He looks really uncomfortable in that suit. "Kip . . . I . . . I want to . . ." And even though he can't finish the sentence, I can tell the words are *thank you*.

I nod and smile. "You're welcome."

The next morning, after the funeral mass at St. Mary's, we process up to Willow Grove for the interment. I'm in the lead hearse, Black Beauty, right next to my dad.

"It was a beautiful service," he says.

"Father Tallman did a nice job," I say. "He always takes the time to personalize the eulogy so it's really special about the person."

"Nanbull's obituary helps with that," Dad says.

A few years back Nanbull started writing obituaries filled with real stories about the deceased person's life. Little memories friends and neighbors had, especially the fond and funny ones. The newspaper charged us a fortune for the space, but Nanbull insisted these stories had to be told.

Nanbull had a dream of being a writer. I say she got her wish with these stories. All of those obituaries she is writing on the people of Clover, Mom is keeping them in an album in the office. Maybe one day they'll make it into a book. I bet every family in Clover would want one.

After the coffin is lowered into the ground and all of the people in fancy black clothes say their final condolences to the Jeffers family, my mother hands Majestic a wicker basket with a bleeding heart plant inside. This is Mom's special tradition. She gives one to every family we serve. The little pink flowers are shaped like hearts and the plant blooms again each spring. They're perennial, Mom says, "like the people we love who live on in our hearts, forever."

"Thank you, Mrs. Campbell," Maj says, and my mother hugs her tight.

Mr. Jeffers invites our family to the buffet lunch at his home. Mrs. Brumbaugh is catering it. Stew is helping her. All of the Campbells, our whole family, we go.

It feels weird standing right near Bub Jeffers, in his dining room, eating macaroni and cheese and Swedish meatballs off a china plate. It feels strange and awkward and uncomfortable, but somehow it feels okay.

Nanbull looks over at me. She nods her head up and down, smiling.

*

Later, it's nearly midnight, I head downstairs and outside. I look up at the sky. I smile. There it is. The ship. Well, really, stars shaped like a ship. I hear a horn.

I feel this good, peaceful feeling inside. *Bon voyage, Mrs. Jeffers. Happy sailing.*

CHAPTER 17

A Golden Matter to Settle

Ev'ry time it rains it rains pennies from Heaven.
Don't you know each cloud contains pennies from
Heaven?

—Johnny Burke, 1908–1964

"Where are you getting this from, anyway?" the man at Clover Stamp and Coin asks me as he weighs the gold egg I found on the beach. I don't know what happened to the clover. I thought I put it right in the same pocket with the egg, but it wasn't there. Must have slipped out somehow.

"Your guess is as good as mine," I say.

"What are you, a wise guy?" he says.

"No, sir, sorry. It was a gift."

The value of gold has gone up in the two weeks

since I traded in the nuggets. The egg is worth nine thousand dollars.

Nine thousand dollars! That's nearly enough for all the improvements Dad needs to do so the State won't close us down. *Yes! Thank you!*

But who am I thanking? Where is the gold coming from? God, is it you?

The man is looking at me like I'm loony.

"Where are you getting all this gold?" he says, suspiciously. "Are you stealing it? I think I better call your parents. What's their number?"

"No, sir, don't. I want to surprise my dad. This money is going to save him."

Biking home, I wonder how to give the money to my father without explaining where it came from. I'm afraid if I tell him I can help the dead, he'll really expect me to take over the business. Talking to the dead would seem like a pretty excellent skill in this field. Then I'll be chained to funeral service forever. I'll never get my boat, sail off with my buddies for the good life . . .

What to do? I need to talk to Nanbull.

I knock, but no one answers. The door's unlocked and I go in.

Nanbull's green canvas shopping bag is off its hook in the kitchen. She probably went to get groceries. I hear Aunt Aggie snoring loudly in her room.

For some reason I feel drawn toward Nanbull's desk.

I pull the little brass cord on the green lamp. The cord bobs back and forth like a buoy. I smile at Nanbull's old typewriter with the eraser ribbon built in for fixing mistakes. When Nanbull heard her typewriter was becoming obsolete, she called the company and bought a box of a hundred eraser ribbons. "That should last me," she said.

I sit down in Nanbull's chair. I run my hands over the alphabet keys, some letters nearly faded away from use.

Not the *k* though. Guess *k* doesn't get as much play as *e* and *s*.

I think about all of the obituaries Nanbull has written here. All of the beautiful stories she's told about the people of Clover, her friends and neighbors. How they lived and who they loved and how they made a difference.

All of a sudden, I get an idea.

I put a piece of paper in the typewriter and line up my fingers on the keys.

Mr. Christopher Campbell
Campbell and Sons Funeral Home
118 Glenn Street
Clover, Massachusetts

Dear Mr. Campbell,

Fifty years ago, your grandfather, Christopher
Campbell, did a very kind and generous thing
for my family. As the story goes, my grandfather
died suddenly, without an insurance policy,
leaving my grandmother, a young woman at the
time, with no income and six children to care for.
There was no money for a funeral, not a penny.

Your grandfather told my grandmother not
to worry. He put on a beautiful funeral for my
grandfather with the finest casket, sparing no
expense.

My grandmother always talked about how kind
the Campbells were. She pledged that someday
when she was able, she would pay him back.

I am one of their twenty-two grandchildren, a
successful attorney here in Boston. I prefer not
to divulge my name for privacy purposes. I hope
you will understand.

Enclosed is the money we owe you, plus interest.
I understand this is what a good funeral costs
these days. Please accept this with our sincerest
appreciation.

Yours truly,

A Grateful Family

CHAPTER 18

Another Golden Matter to Settle

I've dreamt in my life dreams
That have stayed with me ever after.

—Emily Bronte, 1818–1848

When Dad opens the envelope and the hundreds fall out, he says, "Dear God." He reads the letter, sits down, puts a hand over his mouth. He reads the letter again. He counts the hundreds: one, two, three, four . . .

When he finishes, he rushes upstairs to Nanbull's. I rush after him.

"Mother, look at this," he says, handing Nanbull the letter and showing her the money. His back is to me. I am watching my grandmother's face, trying to get her attention.

Nanbull doesn't see me standing there. She reads

the letter, then shakes her head and says, "That's strange, Christopher. I don't recall a family like—"

I wave my hands all crazy in the air at Nanbull, behind my father's back, and finally, *finally* she sees me. I put my finger to my lips. I shake my head back and forth, crisscross my hands like *stop*, mouthing the word *no!*

Dad is still in such shock he doesn't notice me behind him.

"Oh, wait, Christopher . . . *yes*," Nanbull says to my dad.

I sigh a huge sigh of relief.

"This story is beginning to ring a bell now. That's right, there was this family, six kids, I think, and the man died so young. . . ."

I fold my hands together and bow like I'm praying, mouthing the words *Thank you, Nanbull, thank you.*

I leave and head downstairs. I'll talk more to Nanbull later. Right now, I have another matter to settle.

I bike to Golden's Funeral Home. Over on the new side of town. It looks like a country club with fancy fountains and a long line of black limousines out front. I've got something to say to Zack Campbell.

No way is he ever going to hurt anybody or any cat in Clover again.

When I ring the bell, a tall blond man in a funeral director suit answers the door.

"I'm Kip Campbell," I say, in a loud, proud voice.

"Campbell?" He raises his eyebrows. "Michael Golden," he says, thrusting out his hand all curt and businesslike.

I shake it reluctantly.

"What can I do for you, Campbell?" he says.

"Are you Zack's uncle?"

"Yes." He huffs, like *Hurry up, you're wasting my time*.

"I'm in his class. Is Zack here?"

"No," he says, "of course not. We don't *live* here. This is a funeral home."

That was an insult. Golden is looking down at me, like my family isn't good enough because we do *live* in our funeral home.

"People call it a funeral *home* for a reason," I say. "I just wanted you to know that Campbell and Sons Funeral *home* has been good enough for my family for a hundred and fifty years and good enough for the people of Clover too."

He doesn't say anything.

I planned to tell him what his nephew Zack did to Mosely and Pumpkin and Mrs. Elkin's cat, but then I don't. I remember Jupe saying what he heard at the barbershop about nobody in the family wanting to adopt Zack and how this uncle lost the bet. He obviously doesn't care very much about Zack. And maybe if I tell him, he'll send Zack back to a foster home. . . .

"Are you through talking?" Golden says to me. "We've got calls to handle."

I'm waiting for Zack Golden on the steps out in front of school the next day.

"Hey, Golden," I say. "I want to talk to you."

Zack comes over, all smug and sure of himself. "What do you want, Flower Boy?"

"Stay away from me and my family." I speak in a quiet voice, calm but powerful like my dad does, looking him straight in the eyes. "And stay away from my cat and Drew's cat and everybody's else's cats. You hurt anything or anyone I care about again and my friend Jupe's father, Sergeant Johnson, will have your pimpled blond butt hauled into Mass juvie court quicker than you can say 'trick or treat' on Halloween."

Zack smiles, like *So what, is that all you've got?*

"Oh, and I stopped by your uncle's funeral home."

Now Zack looks nervous.

"It's big and flashy, tacky, too, in a *Soprano's* sort of way, but then again, money can't buy class."

Zack looks scared. "You didn't tell my uncle—"

"No," I say. "Not this time. But try it again and—"

"No, man," Zack says, putting his palm up in the air. "I hear you."

"Good," I say, walking away feeling two feet taller.

"Hey, Campbell," Zack calls.

I turn around.

He looks left and right, then back at me. "Thanks, man."

CHAPTER 19

Happy Halloween

Bliss was it in that dawn to be alive,
But to be young was very heaven.

—William Wordsworth, 1770–1850

I ring Drew Callahan's doorbell at 6:00 p.m. on Halloween night. She answers the door right away. She's wearing a red-and-white soccer jersey. My shirt is Clover green.

"Different teams," she says, smiling. "Oh well."

It feels weird trick-or-treating with a girl. Since I could walk, it was always me and Tuck on candy night. Then Stew joined us in first grade. Then when Jupe moved to Clover, he made it a foursome.

I didn't tell my friends about going out with Drew. Tuck knows, but I don't think Stew and Jupe do. I'm not ready for the ribbing I'd take from them. I figure if Drew and I stay down here by the pier, maybe, just maybe, we won't run into them.

Drew grabs two yellow PriceCheck bags for us to use.

I ring the doorbells. Drew says, "Trick or treat." I'm too old to say that.

We rip open the good stuff right away, eating the candy as we go. I trade her a Milky Way for a pack of Skittles.

When we get to the last house I say, "Mind if we stop by Birdie's?"

"Sure," Drew says.

Birdie is surprised, but happy to see us.

"Trick or treat, Birdie!" I shout.

"No tricks here," Birdie says. "No candy either. Wasn't 'specting company. But c'min from the cold and I'll find ya a treat."

Birdie walks off toward a back room. "Sit by the fire and warm yer bones."

Drew looks at me and bites her lip to keep from laughing. I bet the word "bones" sounded spooky.

I move toward the fireplace and Drew rushes to join me, sticking to me like glue. The motion of our bodies sends the paper cranes flying overhead, making a swirl of crazy dark shadows on the old stone hearth.

"They're beautiful," Drew says, looking up at the cranes, her face aglow in the firelight.

God, she's beautiful. I kiss her on the cheek.

Whoa, who knew? My heart is pounding, my palms all sweaty.

Drew smiles at me. I smile back. She brushes some hair away from my eyes. "First time I've been kissed by a rock star," she says. "That's what all the girls at school say because of your hair. Did you know that?"

I smile. 'Rock star' works for me. Definitely better than Flower Boy or Freak.

Drew laughs. "What are you thinking, Kip?"

I'm thinking how I want to kiss you again.

I put my hands on Drew's shoulders and draw her toward me. I lean down.

Birdie is coughing loud. "Here ya go," she says, coming toward us, barely containing a smile. "Found these on the beach. I don't know. Might be worth something."

She hands Drew an earring. It's silver with an emerald stone. "Sorry. Just found the one. Maybe if you look you'll find the other. 'Course, no telling where it came from. Coulda come off that pirate ship off the Cape."

Birdie turns to me. "Here ya go, skipper," she says. She hands me something and closes my fist over it.

I open my hand. It's a gold four-leaf clover.

What? How could that be? Maybe it just looks like the one I lost. . . .

"Is that *real gold*?" Drew says.

"I don't know," I say, staring at Birdie.

Her eyes meet mine, but she isn't giving anything away.

"Thanks, Birdie."

"Yer entirely welcome, Skipper," Birdie says. She nods toward our yellow PriceCheck trick-or-treat bags, filled with candy. "Got any cats in there?"

"*What?*" Drew and I say together, horrified.

"KitKats," Birdie says, laughing. "KitKats. You know, the candy bars."

Drew and I ruffle through our bags and pull out every single KitKat for Birdie O'Shaughnessy.

Happy Halloween.

CHAPTER 20

Lucky

There are only two ways to live your life.
One is as though nothing is a miracle.
The other is as though everything is . . .

—Albert Einstein, 1879–1955

I'm sitting up here on my throne, winter jacket and gloves on, staring out at the whitecaps on that whippin' wild Atlantic Ocean. So much to figure out. Where is the gold coming from? How did Birdie get that clover pin I lost? Is it the same clover or maybe there's more than one? What does it mean? How come I'm the one who can help the dead in Clover? Why did I get picked for this job?

Let the questions roll in and out like the waves, Kip. All will be revealed in time. Some things are a mystery. It makes life a grand adventure.

Who is talking to me?

A dead person?

God?

My own self talking to me?

The wind blows hard against my face.

I close my eyes and take a deep breath. I think about Dad and Mom, Chick, Liz, Mosely, Nanbull, Aunt Ag, and how much they love me. Tuck, Stew, and Jupe, all of us at Guts. Me and Drew trick-or-treating. The KitKats for Birdie.

I'm not sure what will happen next.

I'm not sure if I'll keep helping the dead.

All I know today is that I'm feeling awfully lucky.

And that feels good.

Acknowledgments

With thanks to. . . .

My wonderful Simon & Schuster editor, Courtney Bongiolatti, and especially my publisher, Rubin Pfeffer, who had the great idea in the first place.

My agents, Tracey and Josh Adams of Adams Literary.

Ellen McNulty Ryan and Jack McNulty of Green Island, New York, for sharing what it meant to grow up in a family-owned funeral home and to serve your neighbors with honor for generations. And to the entire McNulty family. You are wonderful people.

My friend Jim Martin of Mount Ida College who introduced me to Dr. Victor Scalese years ago, connecting me with the Dodge Company and so many countless fine professionals in funeral service.

Judy and Steve LeGraw for the blessing bowl.

A certain Vermont inn for the "mouse ladies."

My Irish sister, Kathy Johnson—"put that in your pipe and smoke it."

My dear friends Pauline Kamen and Fred Miller for decades of encouragement.

My writing colleagues, Jennifer Groff, Debbi Michiko Florence, Nancy Castaldo, Rose Kent, Eric Luper, Kyra Teis, Lois Feister Huey, Liza Frenette,

Helen Mesick, Ellen Laird, Robyn Ryan, Karen Beil, and Heather Norman.

My friend Frank Hodge for many inspiring chats at Hodge-Podge Booke.

My friend Debbie Dermady, a book champion and author-nurturer extraordinaire.

My mother, Peg Spain Murtagh, who always signs her name with a smiley face.

My sister Noreen and brother-in-law Mike Mahoney and my nephews, Ryan and Jack; my brother Michael Murtagh and Donnie Reznek; my brother Jerry Murtagh; my brother Danny Murtagh and Liane Terrio; and my brother and sister-in-law Kevin and Colleen Murtagh; nephews, Liam and Brendan; and my beautiful niece and goddaughter, Lauren; Aunt Jane and Uncle Duke Ducatt; Aunt Mimi Spain Hannan; Aunt Virginia Spain Meyer; and all of my wonderful relatives.

Eileen Burton, Lori Goodale, Terese Platten, and Jan Cioffi, my Sage friends forever.

All of the people who have invited me for school visits.

Every teacher, librarian, bookseller, parent, and caring adult who puts a book in the hands of a young reader in the hopes it will be a good match.

Most especially, my sincerest thanks to my readers. I am honored by your letters.

And, always and forever, to my three sons, Christopher, Connor, and Dylan. You are my greatest gifts.

Read on, write on, dream BIG.

Coleen

About the Author

COLEEN PARATORE is the author of The Wedding Planner's Daughter series, *The Funeral Director's Son*, *Mack McGinn's Big Win*, and several other books for young readers. She lives in Troy, New York. Visit her at coleenparatore.com.